Good Blood

Good Blood

K. C. Pastore

RESOURCE *Publications* · Eugene, Oregon

GOOD BLOOD
K. C. Pastore

Resource Publications
An Imprint of Wipf and Stock Publishers
199 W. 8th Ave., Suite 3
Eugene, OR 97401

www.wipfandstock.com

PAPERBACK ISBN: 978-1-5326-5860-0
HARDCOVER ISBN: 978-1-5326-5861-7
EBOOK ISBN: 978-1-5326-5862-4

Manufactured in the U.S.A.   10/11/18

For Kelly Collins and Sandi Glahn
Thanks for your encouragement, insight, and, of course, friendship

CHAPTER 1

Five men dressed in black suits lounged at the far end of the covered seating, hats resting on the table and lungs puffing out cigar smoke. The island of suited solidarity suggested a yang to the drooling, wobbling, prancing children who filled the park. One string-bean of a boy ran his toy train off the table in front of me. His older brother eclipsed the innocent attempt at terror by catching the engine before it hit the pavement. He handed it back to the string-bean with a charming tenderness.

Kids are small. But they take up so much space. They really make a place their own, even the sound space. The buzz of their chatter, peaked by piercing screams, filled out the humid, just-after-rain air.

I'd had my eye on the five men since I arrived with Dad and the boys. I could tell they weren't just the *ragazzi* putzing around after school or work down by the railway station—commonly referred to as *The Joint* due to its joining of the WNY&P, "Little Giant," P&W, B&O and the "Pennsy" railways. The mens' individual appearances didn't vary from the everyday fellow. Back then all the men smoked cigars and wore hats. They all dressed in suits, but the thing is, they never, ever stood in groups.

Those suited fellows took up little space compared to the kids. They kind of blended into the crowd, and their voices sunk beneath the big, picnic rumble. I supposed by their ominous appearance they had been the unlucky recipients of some generational curse. The allure of such a possibility surpassed my cagey curiosity and ignited into full-blown rapture.

In those days the world still fascinated my hazel gaze. People had stories, and they told them—all. A wealthy inheritance of stories proceeded down from generation to generation. Now that inheritance was the only treasure I could count on, so I bet my life on it.

I had heard my fair share of charming, romantic sagas about midnight street races and fantastical tales about how the old men made their ways from Italia to Mahoningtown, Pennsylvania. Even as a kid, I knew that the stories were, at best, only *based* on true stories. The great art of after-spaghetti, wine-drinking tale-telling hinged on the grandiose inflating and deflating of various historical events for the purpose of intoxicating the listeners. Even in the haphazard rhapsody of childhood, we all kind of secretly dreaded that the stories we heard were too otherworldly, too extreme, too good. But we took them for what they were, stories. We dreamed them into existence.

That giving up fact for fiction changed just after I turned eleven. I finally learned how to weave my way through the characters and plot twists. I developed what I thought to be a "good sense" for discriminating between reality and illusion. But it stained me with a haunting sadness.

Gia, my wildly invasive cousin, positioned herself in the human-infested chasm between the five men and me. Gia's hair bounced—incessantly—as she told me all about her new job at Colombo's Ice Cream Stand. Like how she had tried almost all the flavors except for caramel, because she preferred to have caramel on her sundae instead of intermixed with the actual white scoop of paradise itself. Her long eyelashes flitted as she told me about the cleaning procedure for the ice bin, which apparently was agonizing.

"I never feel totally good about it!" Gia exclaimed. "For some reason, the ice bin builds up these little piles of dust around the corners, and then the melting ice cakes them into the corners. The water evaporates overnight, because Johnny makes us leave it open."

Morbid, imaginally constructed images flashed in my brain—crusty, old skin-cell particles, and various other wastes bonded to the sides of the bin.

"And," she continued, "if we use sanitary liquid on it, we contaminate the ice. So we can only use boiling water, which is super hot, cuz our hands are so cold from being in the coolers all day!"

My stomach growled. I tried to shield my imagination from the white paradise. I decided to tune out of the rest of the information she divulged about the internal drama of Johnny Colombo's Ice Cream lest I be scarred and caught hostage in ice cream purgatory, unable to again partake of its divine splendor with full integrity and bliss. Plus, I just abhorred the conversation—monologue—anyway.

A gold flicker caught my eye. One of those men at the far table wore a gold crucifix around his neck. Again, it beamed into my vision. Gia's hair, flapping about her enthusiastic tale of Colombo's or whatever the heck she had moved on to, hid and revealed the refracting sunlight about thirty times a second.

A middle-aged woman in a fitted baby-blue dress sauntered over to the guys. Immediately, the intensity of their conversation ceased. They all sat puffing and looking in different directions. She stood, stroking the back of one of the men's heads. A guy across the table from them leaned forward, swinging his hand about. They all laughed, even the woman. After bending down and kissing him on the cheek, she walked away. That "away" from them, however, was directly toward me.

She walked like cigarette smoke, lazily whipping her feet before her, kind of like a drunk person does. Yet her corset-like posture conveyed that she indeed was in complete control.

I found it odd that I didn't actually recognize that woman or those men. It was the annual family reunion, after all. But if there is one thing that I learned about the world of Italian immigrants, it's that families are so extensive and interrelated you could probably get away with attending any family reunion in town.

The woman continued weaving around small children and unorganized picnic tables. I wondered if she was actually approaching me.

Did they see me watching? I thought.

I looked to her face, but avoided her eyes. Something about her countenance cast a shadow over my sunny mood.

Her vision seemed to be aimed just behind my right ear. She moved closer and closer. Coldness moved up my neck and over my scalp. She got two steps away. I envisioned her reaching down her cool delicate hand to grab my arm and pull me into the rein of her evil glare. Her mouth parted as though to speak. But suddenly, Grandma clunked down besides me and knocked me from my terror. The woman passed behind us.

I realized that Gia was talking at someone else. I wondered how that happened. A sweet fruity warmth drifted to my nose. Grandma held two slices of blueberry pie. They were both topped with a dollop of whipped cream. The massive lump weighed down the roof of the pie, forming a kind of hammock for the cream. Grandma sat a piece in front of me and handed me a fork.

I knew the pie came from Deleone's Bakery. That morning I had seen Mrs. Deleone whipping them up like mad. Popi and I had gone down there to get a donut and shoot the breeze, as they say. Popi still walked along surprisingly well for his age; sometimes I couldn't even catch up with him. His stubby legs swept over the concrete, never stepping on a crack.

Deleone's was only three blocks down Cascade from our house on the corner of Elm. I loved walking down there with Popi. Everybody knew him. He was kind of the "Saint of Mahoningtown." As we walked along, shop-keepers came to their doors to say good morning. Curly-headed women leaned, waving, out of windows, and from their porches stogie-smoking, coffee-drinking men nodded to him. In recent years, Hollywood has tend-ed to portray the 1960s as a mosaic of free-form bliss, which, in fact, aligns completely with my kiddy-brain memories.

When Popi had opened the bakery door for me, it puffed out a sweet canopy of unverified fruit. To my dismay, I'd learned that I had to wait ap-proximately five and a half hours to get a fork-full of it.

Now that plate of long-awaited goodness lay on the paint-peeling table before me. The first bite is always the best, although I probably would have eaten the whole pie if Grandma had let me. Instead, I swallowed a sizable lump of blueberry paste and washed it down with some water. The glint of sunlight caught my eye, again. The five men seemed engaged in jovial conversation.

"Grandma, who are those guys?"

Her face squished together as she squinted toward the crowd.

I pointed to their table. "Those guys. There."

She batted down my arm. Then her bottom lip pushed-up into her firm upper lip and her squinted eyes unraveled. Her head tilted toward me with eyes still on the five men. She placed her right finger up to the side of her nose and proceeded to give it two taps. Over the years I had deduced that guys who got the nose tap were "up to no good." And they were up to a special kind of "no good" that exceeded just regular old "no good," but nobody ever told me the difference. A tacit rule existed banning anyone from asking about things that they weren't told. Dad gave me beatings once or twice, before I finally realized I'd cause a lot less trouble if I kept my damned mouth shut.

One of the men, the one with a nose of distractible size, leaned his head back and let out a howl. Despite his fearsome stature, his laugh honked like one of those dumb seagulls that circle parking lots. Something was peculiar about him, and it wasn't just his missing tooth. When he jerked his head back to laugh, he revealed a thick rosy scar circling the base of his neck.

Grandma swung one arm around my shoulder, while the other nudged my hand to the pie. "*Mangia!*" Eat!

She always did have the tendency to end things melodramatically.

"**A**mbridge—there is a convent in Ambridge," Mrs. Morganson stated. It seemed like she was answering a question for once. Mrs. Morganson really didn't like questions all that much. I think it was due to the fact that she rarely knew the answers. She always, and I mean as-the-clock-tics always, read straight from the catechism, from lesson books, and sometimes pamphlets. That made me wonder if she volunteered to teach CCD for her own sake, since she appeared to know less then the rest of us combined.

"Yes, a convent in Ambridge. They are Franciscan sisters, and they run a school for girls." She sounded fairly confident, even though she recalled the information from her very own brain.

Ah, and there it was. She reached down to a shelf hidden in her podium—a pamphlet. "If anyone is interested, you can read about them." She flipped the pamphlet into the air and then slapped it onto Johnny Primivera's desk.

Mrs. Morganson's voice provoked the internal quake I got when I heard nails on a chalk board. Her nails even did that screech on the board sometimes. Not on purpose—her nails were just so long and thick that when she used a worn down chalk, they dragged along beside her script. I guess she never noticed, even though I would have thought it would feel like driving with the emergency brake on.

That sound provoked in me stomach-turning horror. Her voice sounded like that too. Loud with screechy peaks and tenebrous warbles. I found it both impossible to listen to her and impossible to ignore her.

Charlotte sat in front of me, straight-backed and attentive. Her white short-sleeved blouse had sweat stains at the base of the neck and under her armpits. A tear the length of a pin raveled down her right shoulder-blade. Light blue thread criss-crossed over it, fashioning a string of three stars. That snag happened recently, I supposed, since I hadn't noticed any stars last week.

Charlotte twisted around and set the holy pamphlet on my desk. A smirk crept up her cheeks and her right eye winked. Charlotte made this face a lot. Her eyes seemed to know something that I didn't know. It always made me shiver a little.

I picked up the blue pamphlet.

"School Sisters of St. Francis," I read. Under the title, a black-and-white picture of seven solemn-faced nuns spread to the edges of the page. Four sat, and three stood behind them, all wearing robes and white collars and black hoods. I imagined them gardening together. St. Francis liked to garden. He liked to speak to the animals. I supposed that they most likely did that too.

Mrs. Morganson's rubber-soled shoes clonked down the cement aisle. She stopped beside me and snapped a ruler on the head of Mugga's little brother. It didn't break, but I'm sure it stung like hell. Mugga's little brother, otherwise known as Hog, shot up in his seat. Charlotte jumped. Mrs. Morganson proceeded to screech at him and about him for the final six and a half minutes of class. At one point I saw a tear trickle down Char's face. I rarely saw Char cry, but when she did it likely had to do with someone getting hit. Contrary to Char, I suppressed a smirk. I figured Hog deserved it. I'm sure he, being Mugga's little brother and all, was used to that kind of thing. He lived in, like, constant penance for his family's doomed bloodline.

Mugga was kind of a hoodlum, similar and dissimilar to most of the damned Dagoes, who never looked like he was up to anything good. I would see him walking down the alley behind our house. Grandma saw him once. After peering out the window over the stove at him, she slid the curtains closed. One of them got stuck on the rod, so she got on her tip-toes to reach it. As she yanked, her head shifted back-and-forth, back-and-forth while she clicked her tongue. I couldn't be sure if she disapproved of Mugga or the curtain.

Mrs. Morganson clearly disapproved of Hog. She'd constructed some reason to reprimand him every Sunday since the fourth grade, which is when she started to teach our CCD class. Her badgering didn't end until we got our confirmation and were released from our screech-permeated incarceration.

I tried not to ignore to Mrs. Morg. Charlotte on the other hand watched closely. Another tear dribbled from her eye as she watched Hog get screamed at and hit for the hundredth time. Yet he looked unfazed by the whole shebang.

I flipped open the pamphlet. There were more pictures inside—some of girls in classrooms all dressed in uniform, one of a sister resting her hand on a baby's head, but the last picture showed a nun looking down. A smile beamed across her face, and her hands lay clasped, resting on her chest. A string of beads trickled down the back of her hand. The rosary seemed to have been in mid-swing when the picture flashed. I wondered if she was moving into the frame or out of it.

"You are all dismissed," Mrs. Morganson stated. She marched her rubber-soled shoes up to the front of the room.

Char and I got out the door first. We sprung down the dusty stairs out onto the pavement.

"Ah, there's my mum." She nodded, eyes fixed on a group of women across the street.

Mrs. Pasika stuck out like a sore thumb. Her straight blonde hair was a dead give away that she wasn't Italian.

"You working tomorrow?" Char asked.

"Yea. Just a little in the morning. Popi wants to teach me to click."

She laughed. "What does that even mean?"

I sneered. "It's cutting out the uppers for a shoe. You know—the part that goes around the top of your foot."

"Okay, well . . ." Her downcast eyes lingered and then swung up into a sudden and probably false joy. "That sounds great!"

"It's really important, you know." I always hated when people took shoemaking lightly. That's who we were, the Luces, the shoemakers. "It's almost, like, more important than the sole. I pulled up my Mary Jane whacked the bottom. No body wears a shoe that doesn't actually fit the shape of their foot."

She nodded. "Oh, okay. Yeah, you're right." I knew she cared nothing for shoes. But she always treated whatever I said with an exaggerated seriousness that was never mocking.

We mindlessly jay-walked in silence. Cars never drove through there on Sundays, because it'd be stupid. Parishioners strolled freely from one side to the other all morning. The pattering feet seemed to make the cracked, well-run, downtown streets mumble.

"Can you still ride the line tomorrow afternoon?"

The line. That's what we called our routine bike route around the west side. We made it at least once a week during the school year—Saturdays. But in the summer we biked it every day after lunch. It was just the thing we did, something to get us out of our houses. And riding the line didn't require much thinking or planning, which was nice.

"Well, *yes*, of course!" I answered. "I'll give you a ring, when I finish up. You'll be home right?"

She nodded. "Sounds good. I've got a dance class in the morning, but after that I'll just be at the house."

"No gardening with Auntie then?"

"Good grief! No." Auntie was obsessed with "mending the yard" and "tending the garden," which wasn't all that bad, but her incessant chatter and barrage of questions could tick-off even the noble-hearted Char— which I loved to point out.

We laughed. Charlotte hugged me. We parted ways to our respective surnames.

Angelo, my good brother, stood at the doors of the church, vigorously flapping to flag me down. He had been training quite a lot for the Bholvard Invitational Tri-County Boxing tournament, only three weeks away. His rigid movement resembled that of Frankenstein's monster. To beat people up, you have to get beat up.

Once we made eye contact, he pivoted and hobbled into the sanctuary. After prancing up the stairs, two at a time, I touched the holy water and crossed myself—with integrity. After about six months without a priest, we finally had Father Piccolo, which assuaged my fear of this whole church thing being a big hoax. But we didn't have any nuns, yet. The Mary statue up in the right corner of the sanctuary was the lone, stone, holy mother I could look to in that church. Mrs. Morganson told us that after Vatican II, many nuns left the vocation. I didn't hear why, exactly, only that Vatican II meant something for them. She seemed convinced that that is why we don't see many nuns anymore. But, of course, this came from Mrs. Morg's mouth—words I always took with a spoonful of salt.

The altar boys and Father Piccolo got into formation in the vestibule. I scurried on my toes down the aisle, lest I be caught in the middle of the action. They ushered in the cross and the holy book.

Grandma reached out and yanked my arm, plunging me involuntarily into the pew. The organ blasted out. Throughout the whole stone structure, the grand pipe choir resonated. The high pitches hurt my ears. Grandma told me it was because I had real good hearing, but it still wasn't okay to plug my ears. I learned to endure the shrill peaks of the songs by shutting my eyes and feeling my body rumble with the low, thundering booms.

As much as I actually did try to pay attention, the Ambridge convent floated around my mind for the entirety of Mass. I thought I'd really love to go to that school. The pamphlet said that the girls lived there nine months out of the year while they studied and trained with the sisters. I wondered why Dad hadn't sent me there after Mom went away. I kind of wished he had. I mean, not that Grandma wasn't good company and all, or that Mahoning was a bad school, for the most part. I just thought that would have been better for me, and maybe for Angelo and Nicky too.

I can't count how many times random people said how much I looked like Mom and acted like Mom and rode a bike like Mom and talked about the trees like Mom. She's the one that made me a pure pathetic. Even at that age, I knew I engendered a big pain in the you-know-what for Angelo and Nicky—a constant reminder of her, a remainder of someone who once loved them. I was only five when she went away, but Nicky and Angelo were old enough to remember her more. The way I understood it—they got to have a good memory of her, but I only had myself. And I think she would have been a good memory for them, except my presence wouldn't allow it. I mean, I wandered around slightly reviving her all the time, but never succeeding. She couldn't be a person in the past or the present.

I knew there was some reason Dad kept me around, though. Figured he just couldn't lose two people at once. Or maybe it was because I rolled cigarettes the best.

———————————

Dad shifted the station-wagon into park, and we filed out the back left door. The right door got damaged in a wreck. It still worked, but it didn't work well enough for us to consider it a commodity.

Nobody talked. We all just walked up the path, up the stairs and into the house. I pranced past Grandma up the inside stairs to change my clothes. I never did like dressing up that much—preferred a solid pair of shorts, a tank-top, and saddle shoes, unless I was going into the woods. Then I'd ditch the saddles for some old pair of clunkers that squeezed my toes too tight, a pain I readily endured. I'd do just about anything to keep Grandma from giving me the silent treatment.

I snatched Grandma's Swinger from her bed table and hopped down the stairs. Grandma finally let me have a handle on the cherished camera of hers—literally the only thing I ever heard her ask for. She got it a year back, so she could "record our memories." She really wanted this new-fangled contraption—so she could ruthlessly photograph all of us. But after her health went down hill, she couldn't get out much, which bent her to allow me to take out the thing as long as I promised to come back with records of the places she would never get to go to anymore.

Grandma already had the water boiling for spaghetti. Sunday dinner was at 3:00 p.m., so I had several hours to just fiddle around. I swirled past Grandma as fast as I could, lest she force me into helping her. I opened the back door and, lo and behold, there was Mugga, his back to me, sitting on the step.

He rotated his head and grinned, contorting his mouth to keep a cigarette from falling out. "Hey Rosie!"

While trying to decide if I was going to go back in or just get on my bike and out of there as fast as I could, I just stared at him.

"Where're your brothers?" He looked back to the ground.

"Inside. I dunno what they're doin'" I skimmed past him and straddled my bike.

He snuffed out a couple of breathy laughs. "Maybe you outta go'n check on'em. Tell'm I'm back here waitin'."

"You can knock on the door, ya know,"

"Rather not," he stated, bluntly. There was a pause. He reached back and knocked two knocks on the door. His eyes glared at me.

I cycled away, around the shrubs and onto Cascade. And then something odd interrupted my journey. Just as after I rounded the corner, a whisper came from behind me, "Rosie." I spun around. No one. So I proceeded ahead.

"Rosie!" The whisper came again.

This time I saw a little shrub shivering. A white plump hand shot out. "Help me outa'ere."

I shifted my eyes from side to side. No one else was around except Mr. Primivera rocking on his porch a few houses down. My bike clanked down onto the cement. I grabbed hold of the hand and yanked.

"Ah!" I grabbed ahold of his forearm with both hands, and using my entire one-hundred and five pounds of flesh and bones, I broke a short rather portly human out through the branches.

"Hog! What the heck you doin' in the Lombardo's shrubs?" I demanded.

"Listen here, Rosie," he whispered. He pulled me down, close to his face. "Been followin' Mugga. He'd been goin' house to house all mornin' and then started up again after mass."

"So, what's it to you?"

"Don't know, yet. He's been talkin' to all his friends, but none'a dem been comin' out with'm."

I didn't know Hog all that well, only from school and CCD. He and I were in the same grade and had ended up in the same class the previous year—the "B" class. Char was in the "A" class, the one with all the smart stuffs. But, me and Hog, we weren't good enough. Actually I was surprised to see Hog even in the "B" class. He always had a kind of dumb look about him, not to mention he slept in class all the time, but regardless, when he was awake, he took a liking to talking to me. Couldn't say I really liked him all that much, but then again I barely knew him.

Hog's family was big time in the "biz" as he called it. They were real "big time." I could tell Hog wasn't lying, because on my way to Char's I'd biked past his house on Baker Street—the less steep, though rather lackluster route up Union hill. And Hog's dad always had the latest cars. I mean he, like, changed out cars two, sometimes three, times a year.

"Listen here, Rosie," Hog still whispered, "I gotta feelin' Mugga's up to no good."

"Mugga's always up to no good, dummy."

He tilted his square head to the side and glared his puppy eyes at me.

"Go home, you spud." I swiveled and kept on down Cascade.

I only walked my bike about three yards before hearing short-gaited pattering feet rush up behind me. "Rose, listen here."

"Damn it, Hog. Get outa here and stop snooping around my house."

"I'm on'verge of a real breakthrough, ya see. I think Mugga's turnin' up a new business, been goin' around tryin' to employ people. Been' fixin' up dis garage by r'house, bought a dump truck and all. Been haulin' wood chips and all that for the past week."

"Oh man, well, that's re-e-e-ally something, Hog." I pointed. "Did'at shrub tell ya all that?" I swiveled my eyes forward. "I got to get to the shoe shop. Popi's expecting me to take inventory."

"All right, Rose, all right. I know ur' lyin' cuz its Sunday, and ya just wan'me outa ya hair. Just know 'dis ol'Moon, he came over two nights ago. Gave Mugga a real hard time and ripped his crucifix right off 'is neck." Hog patted two hard thuds on my back and raised his eyebrows initiating a cunning wide-eyed gaze.

Unimpressed, I stared at him. "What's that got to do with me?"

Hog wrapped his arm around my back and leaned close. "I seen ya, Rose." His eyebrows wiggled up and down. "Eye'n up that very same gold chain . . . at the reunion."

"What'r ya talkin' about Hog?" My eyes darted back and forth between his left eye, right eye, left eye, right eye, left eye. The smell of pie. The baby blue dress. The flicker of sunlight. To tell you the truth, I should have just asked Hog right then, who those guys were and what they were up to, but for some reason I found it necessary to lie.

"I seen ya. And, you know what I'm talkin' about. You even asked ur Grandma 'bout the crucifix. I seen ya point at it."

"I don't care about the chain," I lied.

"Yea, well. I'm goin' down to the Joint to check on the location of that very chain." And with that, he stomped his way across the street and down the next alleyway.

The wind picked up. It felt like a nighttime breeze, though it was awfully early for that. But nighttime breeze or not, the way it weaseled through my hair relaxed me. I mean that's the only sane reason I can come up with to explain why I followed him down that alley.

CHAPTER **3**

---

espite Hog's stump-like stature, his little legs could move pretty quick. I've found this to be true of most short people. The tall lanky kind often move slowly, willowy, swaying in the breeze, but the short ones move with crafty agility, weaving in, out, and around any obstacle with ease—yet rather absent of finesse. Eventually, I caught up with Hog, but only with the help of my bike.

We strode up the alley and crossed Elm into another one. "You only take alley routes?" I asked.

"Yep." His face kept forward, focused, and his arms pumped his stocky frame onward.

"Streets're easier, ya know. No gravel. Or weeds. Or crap lying around."

"Nah. Dis is fine."

I hopped off my bike and walked it along. At the edge of the alley, Hog slapped his forearm across my shoulders, like Dad often did in the station wagon when he slammed for a stop sign.

He pointed to my bike. "Set it down," he whispered.

I leaned it against the fence while Hog peered around the corner.

"What's up?" I asked.

"Desolate," he responded.

How the heck did he know that word? I wondered.

The Joint was vacant. In those days, the Mahoningtown train station, otherwise known as the Joint, was the hang-out for the guys. Now, it's just a big patch of grass. Then various assortments of Italian *ragazzi* lurked on its benches and squatted in its shadows—smoking, cussing, drinking and, of course, having a damned good time. I'm still envious of those picturesque scenes I never had the luck or audacity to belong in.

"Wonder where everybody is," Hog whispered.

"Probably at home gettin' ready for dinner."

"Like hell, they are."

Right then, a hoot bellowed up from the river bank that lay just beyond the Joint. A splash crashed and a rowdy crowd laughed and wailed. Hog scurried behind the Joint toward the river.

"Come on." He flagged me over.

I followed Hog, who crawled through the weeds. Grandma's Polaroid Swinger dangled, reckless as a reed in the wind, from my neck, so I tucked it into my shirt. Sporadic piles of clothes lay dumped at the foot of random trees. We crawled right to the edge of the drop-off, and there they were, five guys splashing around in the river.

"Didn't know anybody swam in there," I whispered, "Ang told me there are giant, like eight-foot long, catfish in there. That eat people."

"Well Ang's a liar," Hog assured me. "He might be right 'bout the catfish, but dem guys swim in there a'right already."

Butt naked in a river infested with man-eating catfish.

A sixth guy stood up on the railroad bridge

"Why don't you take a shot of that Rosie?" Hog asked.

I paused. Even from our distance, I could see the moon-shaped scar hooked around the sixth man's neck.

"C'mon, Rose. Might come in handy later!" He winked.

Though I had not a clue what he meant by that, I instinctually pulled the Swinger from my shirt. Leaning up on a pair of Levi's, I steadied my elbows and locked him in the viewer. But just as I hit the button, I felt something like a cold slug sliver onto my elbow, and my arm involuntarily jerked. I looked down. A splash echoed from down at the hole.

"Rosie! What the . . .? You missed'im."

Ignoring Hog the best I could, I angrily flipped my head down to see what had touched my arm. It was that gold crucifix, shiny and a little bigger in person—dreadful. I set the Swinger on the Levis and lifted the crucifix for closer inspection.

"Whoa! Hey!" Hog lurched his meaty hand to my face and snatched the chain and charm from my hand. "When you find'is?" His eyes locked with Christ's like he was transfixed by some dubious magic.

Another splash echoed, releasing Hog from his hypnotic state.

"Well, here," Hog stated. He dropped the crucifix in front of me. "Do yer worst."

I stared at him, confused by the statement.

"Here's 'ur chance. Take it for your own."

"Thought you wanted it," I said. "Ya know, give it back to Mugga." I tossed the crucifix back over to Hog.

"Nah, you gotta take it. You're the one eyein' it up. Ought to have yer own plunder."

"Plunder?"

"Ol'Moon, he gave that to Mugga 'bout a year ago. Wasn't ever really Mugga's." He paused. "I ain't doin' this out of no "what's rightfully ours" kinda thing. Take it, Rose."

"I am not stealing." I had no intention of taking anything.

"It's not stealin'."

"Sure it is. And, stealing's a sin."

"Nobody's gonna know."

"Sure will, haven't you heard of the Father, the Son, and the Holy Ghost, you spud?"

"And." He wobbled his head back and forth and tossed the crucifix back. "What make's dis a sin?"

"Stealing's a sin, cuz you gotta confess it. You do go to confession, right?"

The men joshed back and forth below—throwing rocks and dunking each other like a pile of kids after rain. Then I saw one of them stand on the bank and pull his jeans up onto his waist.

"You goin', Rocky?" one of them yelled.

Hog whisper-yelled at me, "C'mon! They're gonna be finishin' up!" He scooted backward on his hands and knees and pivoted around, cracking a stick, bumping into a tree, and getting slapped in the face by slender branches and elderly weeds.

The hoard of guys swam toward the bank. I froze.

I heard Hog behind me, "Grab it and run, Rose. We gotta split!"

I lifted the crucifix. The man on the cross wasn't looking at me, but I felt like he was. What would Father Piccolo say? Me, willfully sinning, giving into temptation.

"Stealin's not stealin' if the person your stealin' from stole it," Hog told me.

"What?"

"Listen here, Moon stole that chain from a nun."

A nun? This was stolen from a lady of the church, a sister? I lifted the clasp with my left hand. The kind-faced nun appeared before me. Anger bent my stomach in half. I must. I shoved the crucifix into my pocket. Damn him. I must deliver this chain from evil. I grabbed the Swinger and raced toward the fence where Hog was waiting by my bike.

It was good that I stole that crucifix, I figured. At least I would respect it. I saw the holiness in it, the blessed hands of the sister on it.

Hog and I strolled home, unseen by the *ragazzi*, completely at peace. This time Hog led us out onto the street. The safety of society's concrete slabs wrought order. My heart slowed from the threat. The brassy boom of a train's whistle resonated through the thick air signaling the release of yet another shower of soot to settle in the cracks of our sidewalks and pockets of our pants. Whether from the black train-clouds or the luminous plumage of the steel mill chimneys, all this dirt kept us Luces in business. A little shoeshine here or there really does add up in the end.

We approached my house. I headed to the front door, but Hog split at the corner of Elm and Cascade—heading back toward the shrubs from which he came. He said he didn't very much like walking on Elm, always felt like somebody was watching him out there. I had no idea why. Cascade's the street where all the old folks sat out on their porches, house after house after house. I guess what he meant was on Elm he felt as though he was being watched, but on Cascade he *knew* he was being watched. Taking out the "maybe" and replacing it with "definitely" lends some comfort, but I hoped we weren't ever watched.

When I tromped onto the grass, the pungent aroma of freshly sliced blades and newly released chlorophyll burst around me. I loved that smell, although it made me sneeze.

I knew that if Hog ever told anybody I took that crucifix, I'd be dead. I'd be as doomed as a nightcrawler on a sun-baked driveway.

Dinner was as lively as ever. Once you got few a glasses of wine into Popi and Dad, they'd get rowdy. They'd start telling stories and bickering over the parts the other was leaving out. The stories had a tendency to transform themselves from week to week to month to year. I often figured they were quite manipulated, untrue by that point.

We finished the spaghetti. Dad and Popi were going on harassing each other. Angelo and Nicky had even started up. Grandma teetered around the table, inconspicuously delivering elderberry pie onto each empty plate. After she reached around me to pour some wine into my glass, the rosy liquid sloshed into it and swirled to a halt.

Good grief, what have I done? I wondered. My heart still pounded. I ran my fingers over the crucifix, concealed by the material of my shorts and one layer of the inside pocket. It barely formed a lumpy cross. Meanwhile, the stories floundered on from one to another, but I couldn't listen anymore.

And I couldn't bear looking into Grandma's knowing eyes. I wondered if she could see in them the grave sin of which I had willing partaken. I worried that the impossibility of telepathy was insignificant with her. I supposed she always knew what kind of secrets we kept, but rarely did she actually shame me, and never in the presence of the whole family.

After a nerve-ridden train of moral-logic and self-deprecation, I concluded that I must go to the church in the morning and return the crucifix. The likelihood of finding the actual nun was minimal, but indeed the church was her family, a sister of God, so in that respect the piece did belong to the church just as much as it belonged to her.

The conversation unwound. Grandma and I cleared the table and began our ritualistic dishwashing routine: stacking on the right, Grandma washed, Grandma dunked in the clean left-side water, I pulled out of the water, I dried, I stacked in a reasonable configuration. But all the while, though my hands cleaned the dishes, my mind lingered on what I had taken. Grandma dismissed me early; she'd put them away herself.

The night dragged on. Though unconscious, all save about a half-hour, I knew what solemn business awaited me at the coming of dawn. So within a half-hour of its arrival, I peed and then escaped sudden death.

My nimbleness had faltered on the way back from the bathroom. Having memorized all of the squeaks on the stairs, I had placed my feet, meticulously in the various safe-zones. In this manner, I sneaked back up to my room. But suddenly I froze. It had dawned on me that I'd forgotten the eleventh stair. After dissuading the shame, I gathered my memory had failed me due to the nighttime hours and puffy sleep that weighed on my eyelids. I took a deep breath and guessed the best that I could. But of course I stepped exactly on the epicenter of a squeak. And the noise I made was instantly followed by another, right when I made it to the top. Popi had swirled out of his bedroom in a half-wakened haze, and I'd heard a click. His pistol pointed straight at me. My hands swung up above my head.

"Popi!" I whispered, "It's me, Rosie."

He didn't flinch.

"It's me!"

The pistol vibrated in his hand. Then he dropped it to his side. I slowly approached him, careful not to startle. He stood, stiff as a board, staring at the floor, evoking a kind of sleep-walking aura. I took his elbow, pivoted him around, and led him back into his room. After nudging him inside, I shut him in there.

Chapter 4

I made it to St. Mary's by six. And to my total shame, I'd stepped on a squeak—again. I just had to leave it all up to fate.

This wasn't the first time I had made a pilgrimage to the parish at this hour. I liked to pray before anyone else stirred. Grandma taught me how to do that. Though she didn't do it anymore. Her knees got bad enough that she couldn't handle the walk to church, even as flat unadventurous as it was.

I passed through the large stone entry way, entering the Notre Dame of our city, and glided down the center aisle. I heard a wet sucking sound billowing from the walls, only to realize that sound was coming from my own foot. The echo bounced around the four corners of the empty sanctuary disguising for four steps that I had a clearly old, but slightly moist with dew, pile of shit clamped onto my left saddle shoe. Seeing that I stood only about fifteen steps from the door, I slowly backed up, not taking my eyes off of the altar, into the foyer. I turned at the door and jumped into the bushes. By the use of the sharp edge of a rock in the flowerbed I proceeded to scrape the shit off my shoe.

Before I had a chance to notice him, Mr. Carmine Carmidio made his way up the stairs of the church and caught me—seemingly defacing the property of the most venerated church in town. How was I to run those frequent errands for Grandma? I thought I would never be able to face him at the counter of Hyde's drugstore ever again.

Geez, oh man, I thought. Only God himself knows what Carmine thinks of me now. How could I possibly avoid the man though? Hyde's. Man, oh, man.

But to my relief, he politely winkled a little smile, continued into the church, and apparently disregarded my satanic actions.

I put all that behind me so I could appropriately approach the altar. I entered the foyer of the church once more. But . . . holy water? I looked to my right. No holy water. Holy water? I already did this once, so I questioned whether it was taboo to partake and cleanse again. Holy water—period. I needed some distance between me and the dog shit.

I reentered the sanctuary and slipped down the center aisle. Carmine sat at the third row back on the right side. I didn't want to encroach on his space or look like I was stalking him. So I bowed, crossed myself, and sat in the fourth row on the left side.

I thought, Carmine was one of those dull individuals. You could tell by his blank and sentimental face—sweeping his stoop and stocking his shelves and not thinking much at all about life. The thing is, those kinds of people always made me feel a little sad; in fact, they still do.

The sanctuary of that church had a holy scent: lilacs, and fresh oak, and old-people skin. It welled and billowed and swarmed me like it always did. Then, slowly, a whiff of my shoe seemingly puffed into the air and crept into my nostrils—a devastating blow. Shit, of all things, hindered me from drinking in that heavenly smell. I shut my eyes and attempted to smell through the crap. The holy scent remained, though I could barely sense it.

I eased down the kneeler with my unsoiled foot and proceeded to kneel. A pang of lightning shot up through my knee. A couple days prior I had acquired an injury due to my reckless attempt to win a fight.

Angelo had come home with a new pair of boxing gloves—bright red with a gleaming, untarnished gloss finish. They were beautiful. He wrapped the cuff of white leather tight around my wrists. I jabbed into the air. Those gloves glided.

"Light as a feather! These are real nice Ang."

"Yea, I know. Coach gave 'm to me. Said they accidentally shipped an extra pair."

"Wow." I jabbed out a couple times and bounced around. "Now we can have a real fight!" I hit him in the arm. Angelo laughed. "Go," I hollered, "get your other gloves."

Angelo leapt up the stairs. He got really fast at the stairs, ever since his growth spurt. All the men in our family started out short and then had a growth spurt right before they turned seventeen. Over those past three month, Angelo had really shot right up. He was already taller than the average Luce, and now he was way taller. He rose up taller than even Nicky, who, last year, sprinted to five feet, ten inches. I'd say Angelo stood about six feet, maybe even six-one. Regardless, he unfortunately looked rather gangly, all stretched out like taffy.

I tried my best to enjoy the gloves while I had them. Angelo gave me all his old stuff, which means I was now the owner of his old gloves. I wasn't at all unhappy about getting the old gloves. I gladly accepted everything that funneled its way down to me. By funnel I mean Angelo dropping off stuff on my bed. I never saw Ang do it, but Nicky never gave me anything, so I knew it wasn't him. In fact, I kept a special box to store all of the stuff Angelo gave me—baseball cards, caps, notebooks, an old-pocket knife, a fishing lure, an Air Force flight jacket that was rerouted from Popi, and a mint-green super ball.

Now that I had my own gloves we could have a real fight.

Weekly, sometimes bi-weekly, Angelo instructed me in boxing. He started teaching me when he started, a year and a half earlier. But since I was smaller and a girl, he used to give me the gloves. I felt lucky and angry by the whole process, and that was even before I recognized he couldn't actually hit me like he is supposed to, because without gloves, he'd probably break his hand and my face simultaneously. But after I got his hand-me-down, we both had our respective sets of gloves, allowing us to have a proper fight.

Angelo leapt back down the stairs and entered the living room exhibiting his new footwork. He flailed his arms out to the sides and crossed them over each other in front of him, all while keeping up the Charleston-like feet. I stoically watched him approach—that's what I did when I didn't know what else to do. On about the third flail, his right arm swung back so far that he smacked the lamp on the end table. The lamp fringe fluttered to the side as it fell in slow motion. Angelo spun around and caught the lamp before it concluded the leap to its death.

I laughed so hard I had to brace myself on the wall. Grandma peeked her head around the corner from the kitchen before returning to whatever she was doing in there.

Angelo pulled himself together. He began his approach. I struck first. Left, left, right. Cover the jaw, keep the knees bent and the feet active. Stay aware, stay very aware. Deflect. Strike. Keep the feet active. Look in his eyes. Left, left, right. Feet active. Uppercut. Deflect. Take a hit. Respond. Look in his eyes. Stay aware. Stay aware. It would be a lie to say that I didn't notice he was taking it easy on me. Angelo wouldn't have dared to actually clock me a good one, and it's not because he was merely avoiding the guilt he'd feel for hurting his kid sister. He was just kind, that's all.

And that is when the injury happened. I'd dropped, free-falling, avoiding Ang's left hook, and whacked my knee on the corner of the coffee table. The front door slammed shut. I'd ducked, again, under one of Ang's cross-jabs and nailed him right in the gut.

Nicky clonked down the hall and looked into the living room. "Oh, come on. Stop teaching her to fight," he insisted. "She's gonna get herself in trouble one of these days. And, you know how that'll look."

"You jealous? You jealous, Nicky!?" Angelo taunted. "You jealous your kid-sister fights better than you?" He kept bouncing back and forth, alternating feet and brilliantly smiling.

Nicky swaggered past the still-frightened lamp.

"Come on, Nick. Hit me! Hit me, Nicky! Hit me!" Angelo taunted.

Nicky walked up to Ang, and with confident ease punched him right in the face. Nicky slammed him so hard that Ang actually spun in a circle before he smashed up against the mantle. Like ten of Grandma's knick-knacks shattered on the floor.

Grandma shuffled in from the kitchen. "Angi ,what-a happen?"

She knew exactly what happened. Her head snapped over to Nicky.

Like all the Italians did, Nicky extended his hands and hunched his shoulders forward. "What?"

Grandma rested her fists on her hips, what was left of them anyway. She had evolved into a rather symmetrical cylinder.

"He asked me to hit'm," Nicky continued. "So I did. What's wrong with'at?"

Grandma turned to Angelo, extending her hands and hunching her shoulders forward. "You-a break-a the house. You-a be ashame-ed Angi!" She vigorously patted him on the side of the face—not quite a smack, but not exactly lovingly. "Clean up-a!" She shuffled back to the kitchen, her hand flapping above her head all the way.

Ang got back up from the floor. After I retrieved some frozen peas for his face, I lurked near the hallway door for a while, just watching. The room emitted bland badness like a gray cloud on a Sunday. Nicky brushed into me as he left, but Ang raked up all the ceramic pieces. I turned and meandered into the kitchen,

Grandma had her back to me. She was rifling with something. Her arms tensed up and released, tensed and released.

"What you doin' over there?" I asked.

Grandma turned slowly toward the sink. As she swiveled, I saw the secret item. Lo and behold, it was a spray can of whipped cream. She'd been trying to put whipped cream on the pies? This was a big deal. Because Grandma made basically everything herself and wrinkled her lip at any kind of modern innovation. Grandma shook and squeezed that metal can in every possible way, but nothing happened.

"You've got to put your finger over the spout-thing." I gestured. "And lean it to the left or right."

She stuck out her bottom teeth and stared at me.

I made the hand motion at least fifteen times. Then, high-browed and wide-eyed, she put her finger up next to the spout-thing, and *poof!* White fluff, literally everywhere. It went all over her face, my face, the cupboards, the cantaloupe, the clean dishes, and the dish towels. The bottle spun on the floor. It filled up every crevice and chip in the grout. Grandma had pushed the spout-thing with such vigor that she'd ripped that sucker right off.

Cream-covered-face and all, Grandma dissolved into laughter. Her hand grasped my shoulder kind of swinging me about with her own laughter. I started to laugh too. I swiped a bit of cream off of my shoulder and ate it, which led Grandma to do the same.

Everything got dead silent while I waited for her to process the sensation.

Suddenly, Grandma—hand on my shoulder—looked straight into my eyes, her face grave. The pregnant pause had gripped my nerves. Her eyes opened wide and she said, "Isa-good!" We busted out into even greater laughter.

I loved Grandma—the world's greatest optimist. She pretty much always made a good time out of anything, even when she had to rewash the dishes, change her clothes, mop the floor, rinse the cantaloupe, wipe down the cupboards and replace the dish towels. I though it must have been nice to never get angry. I mean, I knew if Popi or Dad were in that kitchen what kind of fire-blazing situation they would create.

––––––––––––

My mind snapped back to the present—the kneeler and my throbbing knee. I found it a real pain in the you-know-what to think I went through that whole fight with Angelo only to acquire a bruised patella. Nicky, on the other hand, just waltzed in and took the prize.

Guess life's like that, I muttered to myself.

Luckily the kneelers were comfortably padded in St. Mary's Church, unlike the cracked old wood ones at Madonna's. I opened my eyes and looked ahead to the silent altar. The church was perfectly still, save two crows having an argument outside. I scanned over the pews. Carmine no longer sat up ahead of me. I concluded that he must have left when I got lost in the covering of whipped cream.

Footsteps echoed. I glanced over my left shoulder as two men entered a pew several rows back. Their olive skin and thick raven black hair gave them away—Sicilians. Both wore black suits with white button-down dress shirts. Italian guys who came straight from the Mother Land always left the top two buttons undone, making way for a plumage of rich and horrifying, black chest hair. American-born Italians kept their chests covered. But, what could I say? I too was Sicilian, and Popi was one of those chest-hair exhibitionists.

I looked back again. The Sicilians sat oddly close, that is, close to each other. They weren't kneeling or anything and they really looked out of place, not praying and all. Besides solemn prayer, I couldn't work out any other reason a soul would enter a sanctuary at that god-forsaken hour.

I kneeled. They sat behind me. I shivered at the thought of them staring straight into my back. The clunk of my swallow and that weight sinking down, down in the pit of my stomach told me they knew I had the cross and chain and finally I was about to meet my own foreboding retribution. Soon enough, I found myself wrapping up my prayers so I could get the hell out of there.

Grandma insisted that I light two candles in front of Mary every day, one from me and one from her, since she couldn't make it down there herself. Luckily, my route to Mary and back down the side aisle totally avoided the men. I had deduced a great likelihood of their "being up to no good," which radiated from their imposing, irreverent postures—inappropriate for inside a church. So, keeping my distance seemed wise. I stood, crossed myself, and proceeded toward the altar. As I stood, the cool, metallic crucifix touched my chest. I had it draped around my neck and tucked into my shirt. Surely only one thing was true; those guys could not see me with that chain. My mind raced to find a way to get it off.

I stepped forward. A pair of familiar shoes caught my periphery. Carmine Carmidio hadn't left after all. Beneath the horizon of the pew to my right, there he lay, flat on the pew, face down, stiff as a board. I would have thought he'd died, but I hadn't heard him fall. I tried not to think about it.

I tried to continue my slow pace to Mary and proceeded to light the candles—without looking like anything was off. I stretched up to the top, back row, as most people never lit the candles there. As I did so, I held my shirt close to my stomach to avoid being lit on fire. But even though I tried to avoid the flame, one of them licked my right elbow. It took a second to notice it, because elbows are not exactly the most sensitive part of the body. But then . . . I saw. Flames! I threw down the match and flipped my arm over. A very light pink patch already formed at the tip. My attempt at inconspicuousness was drastically failing. I could feel their eyes. The wick's smoke swirled into the air, and with a surge of enthusiastic dread, I turned down the side-aisle, breaking into a sprint. I didn't care what those *dagos* thought. I'd already called attention to myself multiple times. There just wasn't much to hide anymore.

Just after I passed the confessional, the door opened behind me. I tripped over my own foot and slammed onto the whirling gray, marble floor. I immediately shot up and beetled to the door.

"Are you all right?" a man's voice asked.

I spun around. It was Father Piccolo.

"Yeah, I'm fine." I proceeded my scuttling out the door.

"Did you fall?"

"Yeah." I entered the vestibule and leapt out the doors.

My knees didn't start aching or my elbow burning until I had peddled halfway home. All that adrenaline wore off. And I could feel something again.

I peddled onto Elm. When I rounded the corner, I could see Dad and Angelo. Angelo stood, arms folded, on the grass next to the tool box, looking down at the bottom of our '57 station wagon. Dad rolled out from under the car on his little red creeper. It wasn't all that unusual to see Dad rolling around under that dusty-brown piece of junk at least once a week. Basically, something was always wrong with it, and my guess is he also just liked rolling around.

I hoped off my bike and walked it over, my saddle shoes slapping their way across the concrete. As I got closer I could see the blackness of their hands and the sweat swelling on the base of their necks.

"What's goin' on?" I yelled as I made my way up the sidewalk and landed beside Angelo.

"Brake line," Angelo said.

"Ah-h," I nodded, arms folded, as I stood on the other side of the tool box from him. I had no idea what that meant. But judging from the slight edgy quality of Angelo's answer, I decided not to ask. I found that it is better in times like those to just keep my mouth shut. But I stood there for a few more seconds, acting like everything was normal. When the silence continued, I figured it was in my best interest to split.

I ran up the stairs and swung around the banister to effectively launch my body into my room. I jiggled open my dresser drawer, which had a tendency to get stuck at about two inches open. The drawer lurched open so hard the whole dresser clanked around. The lamp on top tipped from side to side like a sailor home from sea. But before it even had a chance to think about leaping off the dresser I seized the base and brought it, seemingly, back to sobriety. Dad's voice in unformatted syllables pounded on the window. After grabbing a pair of shorts from the drawer, I scooted over to the pane. As I slid off my nice shorts and slid into my play shorts, or in this case work shorts, I leaned toward the window to see what was going on.

Angelo had rolled himself from under the car. And Dad was crouched down with one of his hands supporting his weight while the other flailed around like a chicken with its head cut off—honestly. It takes forever for chickens to die. That past spring we visited Mom's sister's family's farm out in Butler. Yeah, glad I lived in Mahoningtown—that's all I got to say.

I squinted, trying to see Angelo's face as he lay there on the ground. Black crap and anger all over it. Then both of them stood up and started screaming at each other. Hands flew all over the place.

Nicky came out from the house across the street and calmly made his way over to the two raging *dagos*. Hands in pockets, he moved his head back and forth while the other two stopped their ruckus and listened. Then Dad put his arm up around the back of Nicky's neck. Nice like. While patting Nicky on the chest with his free hand, he continued yelling at Ang. Angelo didn't seem to take this very well. He threw the tool across the yard and stormed into the house. Next, he slammed the door to the bathroom. I rushed away from the window and continued getting ready for work.

Nicky was Dad's favorite, and to the rest of us, that was obvious. I didn't mind it much. It's just how it was. It's just Italian fathers and sons. Nicky was the oldest, so he was the favorite—plain and simple. Just like Mugga is his Dad's favorite, and Marco is his Dad's favorite and even Dad is Popi's favorite. Plain and simple. But for some reason Angelo just didn't get it. I never did understand why. Instances like that forced me to notice that Ang was just a big baby. He took stuff too personally, especially stuff that Dad said. I never had a problem with it; it's just the way it was. But, then again, I disregarded any ridiculous expectations of Dad. I didn't think he had many emotions. I sensed that we were alike in that way. But when it came to Dad's own opinion, disregarding the whole "favorite" systems, he really did like Nicky the best of us.

I heard Angelo's muffled stomps thudding up the carpeted stairs. When he stepped onto the landing, he slammed his palm against the wall next to his bedroom doorway and slammed the door to his room.

"Ang?" I walked across the hall and knocked on the door. "Ang?"

Silence.

"Ang? You . . . you there?"

"Enough Rosie!" he shouted. "Enough!"

I didn't have any more words than that. My hand dropped to my side and I turned back to my room. I couldn't do anything anyway. I slipped on my shoes and started my way over to the shoe shop.

After spinning around the banister at the bottom the stairs, I saw that the back door was open. Just wide open, letting in all the flies. And through the opening, Nicky's and Dad's bulbous, strained voices rippled from the front yard: RADIATOR . . . MUFFLER . . . PIECE OF SHIT CATALYTIC CONVERTER . . . and a dozen other crashes of godawful car jargon that I'd never get to know, because I was a girl, and therefore stupid when it came to logic or mechanics or business. And to think that these babbling *dagos* were the specimens of the "practical" gender sickened me. A fly erratically buzzed back out the door.

"Rosemary?" A strange voice emerged from the living room.   •

Wide-eyed and quizzical, I slowly walked toward the living room and the voice. It was Mugga, sitting in there, rocking on Grandma's rocking chair and smoking a cigarette. On the couch, Moon sat opposite of him. A puff of smoke billowed from his nose.

"Ang home?" he asked. Another puff escaped when he spoke.

I just stared at him.

"You stupid, girl? I asked is yer brother home?"

I wondered if they were in there when Ang came stomping up the stairs. I wondered if they were sitting there when I walked up. Grandma emerged from the kitchen with a tray of *pitzels* and a cup of coffee.

"Umm. Yeah," I answered. "Yeah, Ang's here."

"Well, go get him."

Grandma set the coffee next to Moon without a word. I plodded back up the stairs.

"Ang?" I knocked on the door again.

"Rosie! I said get the hell out of here!"

"Uh. Mugga's here for you. And, um, another guy."

This time I ran down the stairs and sprinted out the back door, leaving it open. When I turned out of the alley onto Cascade, I slowed to my usual pace. It wasn't my usual M.O. to muse on such events, but Moon's arrogant eyes and Mugga's silence spired on an unavoidable trail of uneasy hunches. A couple of women with grocery totes passed me. I kept my eyes down. The one with the baby-blue smock brushed against me, and I feared that some kind of telepathy transferred skin to skin, and that she knew.

I spun into the shoe shop. And the little bell dinged.

Char and I rode the Line, as usual. Our items of discussion included berries, the upcoming *festa* of St. Peter and Paul, and the likelihood of Donnie Vincini becoming a conspirator with Satan himself.

That evening after I finished my bedtime routine, I opened the bathroom door and proceeded to start up the stairs. The TV murmured in the living room. Its lights flashed shifting scenes on the dingy mauve walls and cast long shadows to my feet. Dad reclined, sideways, on the couch, spitting cherry pits into the ashtray on the end table. Remembering my glass of water, I swung back around and headed to the kitchen. But before I got there, I happened to glance at the back door—something of a sixth sense, one might call it. The door was shut, and locked, but something shuffled around on the gravel outside. It sounded bigger than a cat. I ignored it—mainly to assuage my own fear. To me every sound in the darkness was most likely Frankenstein's monster and therefore ought to be disregarded before seizing me with its imaginative power.

I topped of my water, perfect, and slurped off the meniscus. I decided to drink it down about an inch, before I attempted the stairs. When I strode back out of the kitchen, I peeked over at the back door. The hinge side of the door gapped open about a half-a-centimeter. Just above that bottom hinge, and in that crack, gleamed a little white sliver. Dad sat silent, minus the rhythmic ding of cherry pits. I walked over to inspect the sliver. Its third dimension revealed that the sliver was actually an envelope, a little white envelope sealed by a circle of red wax. Dad coughed. Alarmed, I sprung straight up. Then the back door flung open, smacked me against the wall, and sent my glass of water flying back into the kitchen. Nick emerged from the darkness, and Ang followed him. I slid the envelope into my robe pocket.

Nicky stiff-armed me into the wall when he passed on his way to the living room. "What are ya watchin' in'ere?"

Without acknowledging my existence, Angelo slunk past and started to his bedroom. The glass didn't break. And even though water evaporates, I wiped it up and flung the dampened dish towel over the faucet. I took a swig of the remaining water, and decided on setting the glass back in the cupboard. I mean, it was only water.

Before I climbed the stairs, I snagged an empty toilet-paper roll from under the bathroom sink. I had been saving the empty rolls under the sink for some time—eleven cardboard cylinders tucked beneath the drain pipe. I thought that I might make some craft out of them one day.

Once in the safety and privacy of my own room, I clicked on the light next to my bed. The bright red seal displayed two short swords, or big knives, enclosed by a circle. I ripped open the flap around the seal, so that the seal itself remained securely connected to the envelope. Inside, a message was scrawled on the inside flap of the little card.

In red ink: Family is everything.

That's an odd note, I thought. Family meant a lot to all of us around there. I wondered why someone thought we needed reminding. Neither the envelope or card had an address on it, nor a name. It didn't say who it came from or who it was meant for. The only logical conclusion led straight to Mugga. Like Hog said, Mugga had, after all, been wandering around town up to something, however I couldn't seem to conjure why he would leave such a note. Perhaps it was the slogan of his new trucking company or whatever—quite possible, but that letter being wedged in the door frame seemed too glaringly ominous.

I slipped it into the toilet paper roll and tossed it into my box-of-Ang's-hand-me-downs. It landed beside the crucifix, which I had stored in there once I got home from the church that morning. The chain only brought me bad luck, a sign of the *malocchio,* the embodiment of a curse itself. It was just too dangerous to carry around.

I couldn't sleep too well after finding that letter. I wondered why somebody put it there and who exactly it was supposed to be for. Family is everything? Part of me wondered if Hog slid it in there. But, that couldn't be right. I'd seen the kid's hand writing, and it was shit-in-ditches, comparatively. He'd be the one to write something like that though, especially after all of that talk about his brother starting a business and all of his snooping around to keep an eye on everyone.

I awoke from a dream in the middle of the night. In it I was a dangling from a grape vine, hanging on the tip of a cluster of grapes, a grape among grapes. The other grapes were Angelo, Nicky, Dad, Grandma, and Popi was at the top, by the stem—a little cluster of grapes trapped, tiny, under leaves in the middle of an eternal row of vines and clusters—stuck.

I guess I never thought too much about everybody else's family. Our street filled up like little clusters of grapes along a path. Maybe I kind of opened up to the world a little bit that moment. We were just one cluster in a very big interconnected vineyard. That's what it felt like at least. And it felt far from good.

I heard some kind of noise, so I rolled onto my side and faced the window. The sound was so slight that I didn't know where it came from, if it was in my room or a mile away. That's when the hot fear exploded through my veins. All my muscles seized, and my eye darted around the room. The curtains fluttered with an incoming breeze. The sound was clearly steps, shoes gliding along the concrete beneath my window. It was a man I could tell, by the pattern and weight of the steps. They moved slower and slower. And I knew, without a shadow of a doubt—it was him, finally coming to get me—Frankenstein's monster. He would come for me I knew it. He had come to reward me for my sin. I thought for a moment about grabbing that crucifix and just launching it straight out the window, but I couldn't, I had to see him first, see him with my own eyes.

My eyes were zapped of all moisture. I managed to blink, but only one eye at a time so that I could stay aware and ready for his entry into my room. Wait. That wasn't logical. I was upstairs and he was outside.

A dog's yip from down the street echoed between buildings and houses. The steps stopped. Only a whisper of wind could be heard. I waited. Nothing. Nothing.

I managed to pull the covers off of my legs. I needed to make sure that he wasn't there, that he had moved on down the street. I quietly moved my legs over the edge of the bed. I thought for a second that he might be under my bed, but knew that it was impossible. I stepped onto the floor and toe-heeled steadily toward the window . . . into the ominous light. My finger resting on the sill, I slowly bent toward the open air, praying ever so fervently that he would not be standing down there looking up at me.

CHAPTER **6**

"I found one!" Charlotte's voice echoed across the field. Her arm waved like a white flag of surrender—embarrassingly swooping side-to-side.

I trudged through dewy field, making my way to see Charlotte's treasure and holding Grandma's Polaroid Swinger high above my head so that it wouldn't even graze the tops of the grass. My wallet-size leather pouch, which I'd slung across my shoulder, already contained three arrowheads. I had all the luck that day.

Charlotte opened her grasp to reveal a finely-shaped triangle with little scalloped ridges on the sides.

"Yep, sure looks like one to me." I took the treasure, cleaned it off on my shorts and handed it back to Char. "Okay, hold it out like this." I snapped a picture and tossed the artifact into my satchel. When the camera spit out the black rectangle, I handed it to Char. "Here. You can peel it."

Char gently pulled back on the black film. "O-o-o-h. Perfect!"

I tucked the photo in my satchel with the arrowhead itself.

Covert's field was the best place for these types of expeditions. There used to be a lot of Indian camps down there, along the Mahoning River. Beneath that very field rested an ancient Indian burial city, so they said.

It's always best to go searching for arrowheads there just after it rains. The water raises up from the ground all of those buried treasures.

The high sun glistened off the meandering river. The roar of a distant truck upon a gravel drive had Charlotte peering toward the echo's epicenter.

"That's probably the guy who lives in the log cabin we passed on the way down." I remarked.

The man's name was Richie Covert. His family had lived down in those wild parts since the crash. That is how the bridge there got its name, Covert's Crossing. People didn't frequent those parts though, only if they needed to go to Hillsville or Edinburgh or, God forbid, Youngstown. The only reason that I personally knew the area was because Dad used to take Nicky and Angelo out to those parts for hunting. That was back when Angelo hunted. Angelo and I were great pals, but I honestly couldn't understand his indifference to nature. He avoided the woods. So Nick and Dad were the only ones who'd go out there.

They never brought me. The way I found the place was by following Nicky one morning. He was going to check his traps. Of course, my trailing Nicky lasted only for about three miles, which is actually successful given that Nicky had the ears of a hound and the sense of an Indian. He found me right at the break of the field and the forest after my foot had busted a small stick.

I think I followed Nicky down because I thought it would lead me somewhere. After that quite remarkable three-mile stalk, I considered the possibility of working for intelligence in the national government. Then of course, just before dawn broke, Nicky found me trailing him—due to the stick. I wouldn't be surprised if he knew I was trailing him all along.

At the time of that incident, Nicky was walking on the open tracks, and I followed him about three feet into the woods. We'd just made it to the part where the tree-line left of the tracks panned out into more sparse patches; meanwhile, the tree-line right of the tracks grasped onto an overgrown, cliff-like region. I was on the right side, heading for the scraggly cliff. I remember being pissed with myself for choosing to sneak along that side of the tracks. But now, in retrospect, how could I have known that I was walking into such a splendid trap?

After I cracked that stick, I slipped down onto my side and yet remained nearly upright, given the steepness of the hill. I watched Nicky stop, set down his bag, and just stand there for like five minutes. Then he slowly turned around and came straight toward me. Nick never made any fast movements. He stayed completely calm most of the time. On the other hand, Angelo must have gotten all of the energy in the family. He always flipped around like a bass out of water. Angelo always had to be doing something, anything—some kind of project or plan. Nicky wasn't like that at all.

Nicky came right up to the bush. He reached straight through it and grabbed my arm. With one motion, he yanked me out right onto the gravely tracks. He turned back around and picked up his bag.

"Come on," he said reluctantly, while he continued his walk.

We hiked down the tracks side by side. I balanced on one of the rails—walking on a tight-rope.

"Nicky! Don't I look like the lady over Niagara?"

"Uh-huh," he agreed without looking.

I wasn't real sure if he was annoyed or indifferent—not to the Niagara thing, but to me being there, in general.

We started into the tall grass. The low clouds hung in the sky, tempted to spit. The blue morning-light breathed behind the gray Pennsylvania sky, like a secret color, a more hopeful depth.

That's when Nicky told me that this field was exceptionally good for arrowheads. He said that a lot of Indians fought in a war here and that you could find lost arrowheads everywhere. We cut our way through the kind-of African savanna. He told me it was an Indian burial ground too. I thought I heard the rumble of an elephant stampede in the distance. Then a train zoomed past.

The birds were almost awake by the time we got to Covert's Crossing, the actual bridge itself. We made our way up its steep incline and onto the flat one-lane surface. My eyes laid hold of an excellently dreadful path that lay before us. From that point on, I caught glimpses of Nicky every thirty seconds, when I briefly glanced up. The old one-lane bridge had no walkway. I wondered what would happen if a car came. The 1.5-inch slats of wood that lined it didn't look very stable for a person, let alone a car. The slats spaced out, grossly uneven and often missing up to even three or four at a time. Nicky, about fifteen steps ahead of me, skated along. His feet missed every gap even though his eyes looked out over the river.

I was pretty sure that I was about to fall to my death. Meanwhile, Nicky confidently tread across the abyss leaving not even a shred of fear behind to comfort me.

Eventually, we descended from the bridge. I was just happy to be on dry land again. Nicky hadn't looked back at me since the middle of the field.

I followed him off the road and into the woods—Nicky quiet, me quiet. Then Nicky stopped and pointed out some leaves to me. To my surprise he actually explained which ones were wild ginger and which were garlic and which grow by garlic and how to identify poison ivy and how that is different from poison oak. I was startled, as this was the first time Nicky talked with me, but unfortunately, to me the forest was pretty much one big pile of green. I tried to understand. He pointed out trees, naming their kinds and qualities. And he even pointed out flowers. He told me about a place that was a little north, an abandoned house surrounded by a field of lilies.

Nicky and I never did have much in common. Both of us were too quiet. We just never really talked. Not to mention I was just kind of scared of him, him being my big brother and everything. I think that day at Covert's, Nicky outdid himself in words. It was the most, to this day, I've ever heard him talk, and to be quite honest it wasn't really what I expected to be going on in his brain. From the look of his face, consistently pissed, I had assumed that he only thought about hoodlum stuff.

At Covert's, it felt like maybe he didn't mind me so much. It felt like we were family. It felt good.

Charlotte and I continued our inspecting of the field, but our efforts yielded nothing new. We got pretty close to the train tracks opposite the river.

"Char, let's head back the other direction. I don't think we are going to find much here," I suggested. "I don't think the overflow from the river reaches here, so it's not going to bring up stuff that's buried." When she didn't respond, I looked up at her.

She stood frozen. "What's that sound?"

The train tracks were buzzing bees. Their rumbling matched their vibrating heat waves. I told her, "Trains comin."

With a surprised eye and knowing smile, she challenged me to a race. Charlotte took off toward the river. I grabbed hold of my satchel, and my camera and started after her. The still dewy sheaves of tall field-grass sliced my legs as I cut through them. The grass slowly engulfed us to shoulder height, which made it impossible to see the ground, especially moving at such a rapid pace. I could see Char's head bobbing about ten feet in front of me. Then her head dropped right out of view. I attempted to slow my full speed, but it wasn't quick enough. With arms slicing like windshield wipers through a thick patch of grass, I had both legs simultaneous knocked out from under me. Mid-air, my stomach lurched its way into my lungs while my head and shoulders still thought they were running. After about a half-a-second of total body flight, I face-planted into the ground, holding both the satchel and the camera in front of me, unharmed.

Charlotte lay laughing behind me, and the train zoomed by with an organ-like univocal tune.

"What in the world are you doing?!" I shouted, half playful, half furious.

"I tripped in a little dip or something," Charlotte chuckled. "I was just getting back up, until crazy came barricading through!"

"Well, at least I had my hands out in front of me, before you gave me a lift, or I probably would'a smashed this damned camera."

"Geez, sorry."

After checking to see that the arrowheads were safe, I fumbled around in the grass, acting like I had resumed looking for more treasures. Honestly I wasn't really looking. I was just looking like I was looking and trying to get over my embarrassment. I really hated looking stupid, because I was worried people would start thinking I was stupid all the time.

The train chi-chonk chi-chonk chi-chinked behind us, slowing its pace as the engine prepared to pull into the Joint.

"Hey," Charlotte whisper-spoke. "I think I found something."

"Arrowhead?"

"No." Her voice wavered. She held her finger to her lips to shush me. "Rose, come look."

I scuffled through the grass. Charlotte, bent-over, hands-on-knees, looked to the ground. I went around her to see what she was inspecting. She reached her hand down and moved a creamy colored stick that was encrusted with dirt. I got onto my knees and removed a clump of soil.

"Hm-m," I picked up the stick and examined it.

Charlotte picked up another one. The train whistled in the distance, probably arriving in Mahoningtown. The little two-inch stick was most definitely a bone.

"Looks, like we found a grave," I whispered. "I think these are finger bones."

She nodded. "That's what I was thinking." Char's face started to lose a little color.

Little finger particles were scattered at the base of a garbage-bag sized rock. I motioned for her to help me push it over.

We heaved the rock a solid six inches, enough to reveal the arm and shoulder of a full-on corpse. At first we stared, mouths agape. After a few seconds, I used my foot to kick up the humorous bone a bit. The length of the bone detached from the rounded joint on the elbow end. And maggots slithered out from the bone, leaving dark tracks of marrow over the creamy surface. A horrid stench, far beyond mold, far beyond feces, permeated the air. Terrified, but trying to remain calm, I looked up at Char's face. "I'll bet this is just one of the Indian graves that rose up from the flooded river." I knew better, but I was trying to sound reassuring.

Char's face was now the color of limestone, hard and white. Right before my eyes, all of the color retreated from her lips.

A deep, raspy, yet blood-curdling scream pierced my ears. But the scream did not come from Charlotte, or me for that matter. It came from someone somewhere in the field behind us. At the same time the scream broke out, Charlotte's knees buckled and her forehead smashed right into the rock.

"HE-E-E-LP ME." The voice pleaded—a man's. "OH, GOD."

I dropped next to Char. Her body rolled to the side, right into my arm. Her eyes opened unevenly, and rolled back inspecting her lids.

"A-G-H-H-H!" That scream again was followed by the sound of grass shuffling, met with grunts and the disoriented treading of struggling boots. Someone yelled, "STAI ZITTO GIDRUL'!" followed by an ear-splitting heavy snap. And a grown man's whimper.

My heart pumped blood into my ears and pounded at the surface of my temples. I slowed my breathing and laid my head down on Char's chest. Her heart pounded against my brain.

It sounded like several men were struggling their way toward us. They wrestled about twenty yards away, fifteen yards, ten yards. Grunting, they seemed to be trawling a catch through the mire. I sunk down harder into Char and lowered my hips into the mud, trying to disappear into the ground.

"What the hell?" one asked—a familiar voice.

"It's the ground, gidrul'!" another answered. Their feet made a sloshy sound that told me they'd stepped into a mucky tributary.

"Go down that way, so you can actually see your feet," one told the other.

The sound of their caravan moved to the left of us. They went toward the river. Their voices distanced a little, and I could no longer make out distinctly what they were saying.

Char lay unconscious. I lifted my head from her chest and straightened my arm, lifting my own body. My arm felt real weak. Crawling over

Char's body, I slapped my hand onto the rock, slowly moving the rest of my weight onto it.

The men now seemed a safe distance away. I heaved my weight onto the rock and peered through the thinning tops of the grass. I could see their figures down by the edge of the river.

A siren echoed in the far distance. A fire truck blazed its horn. Or maybe the police. I hoped it was the police. The men started to argue, but I couldn't make out what they were saying. I could see two men from the shoulders up. They shouted at each. One shouted in Italian, but too fast for me to catch.

"AG-H-H-H."

That scream—the victim was barely alive. I ducked my face down to the rock again.

"Scream all you want you ugly bastard, no one's gonna find you!" the familiar voice said.

I looked up again to see if I could recognize the bearer of the voice or find out who was screaming. And I saw the two men pull up a bloody fellow. One man slammed him up against a tree. The other punched up him in the stomach. I felt my eye start to tear and dropped my head. But I had to know what was happened. I looked back up. The older man that punched him wore black dress-pants and a white T-shirt.

My eyes cleared and all of my senses came together. I saw and heard and smelled better than I ever could, ever before. It was like super-sensing. The leaves greener. The dew crisper, the ground harder. And I sucked in every detail.

The young guy wore jeans. Mud sprawled up his left side. His white t-shirt had cuffs around his biceps, and a gold chain glimmered around his neck. He grabbed the hair of the bruised man and slammed his head against the tree. I couldn't recognize the bruised man. His dark hair, slim waist, and broad shoulders could have been anyone that I knew. His face was too bloody to really see well.

"Well, finish him off!" the other guy shouted. "You want this, Fists, or what?"

The young man slipped a long, slender knife out from a sheath at his thigh. By some supernatural involuntary movement, I lifted my camera to my face. He turned and looked out over the river.

"Prove it."

I clicked.

Through the lens, I saw the side of his face, I saw him. I knew him, but I couldn't believe what I was seeing. Such an event would be too other-worldly, too wicked, too horrifyingly true. Though my brain identified him, some other part seized it and coated it with wax. The vision itself turned into a memory in hiding, a secret too inconceivable for my own young mind and too dreadful for my heart.

He turned back around, and with a swift stroke, sliced the man's throat. Blood spewed. I fell down onto the rock. I could hear the victim choking, a gurgling, muddy cough.

The black rectangle emerged from the camera. My mouth tasted like acid. My stomach heaved in and out. My hands trembled as I slipped the photograph into my pouch. I rolled on my stomach. Vomit cascaded down the far-side of the rock. It puddled around the humorous bone. Compelled to see—I pushed myself back up from the rock and watched. I wiped my mouth on my sleeve. They tossed the body into the river. My fingers were pulsing as they gripped the rock and my sweat dripped down onto them. And, the two men ran along the bank headed for Covert's Bridge about a quarter-mile away.

CHAPTER 7

Charlotte's mouth moaned. Her eyes had rolled back to standard. She looked up at me half-quizzical, half-dead.

Arms still shaking, I swung myself around and sat down on the rock, "Have you ever passed out before?" I could hear my voice warble.

"Huh-uh." She brushed off some of the moist dirt that had stuck to her arm. "What just happened to me?"

"I'm guessing that's a no?" I said, before a let out a smile.

She looked at the trail of mud down the front of her shirt and shorts. "How'd this get here?"

"You passed out after you saw the Indian bones. Then you kind of rolled onto your back."

"I think I remember hearing someone screaming."

"Hm-m."

"Yeah. Who was yelling? A man . . . ."

"Oh hm-m. I didn't hear anything," I lied. "Maybe you just imagined it after you saw the bones. I mean, you got pretty pale before you actually fainted." I can't really put a finger on what it was that moved me to lie. It surely was more biological than cognitive. That kind of compulsive lying is a freedom of childhood alone, and, of course, uncivilized adults, I suppose.

Charlotte sat up and looked around—getting her bearings, I assumed. I glanced back over my shoulder. I watched as the killers darted over Covert's rickety one-lane bridge and rushed into the forest. Sirens blared in the distance.

"I think we ought to call it a day," I said, "I think we've had enough adventure. What do ya say?"

"Yes, let's head back," Charlotte stood up and stopped to listen. "Gee, those sirens seem really close."

We both stood, our backs toward the river. A plume of smoke gathered in the sky, not even a mile away.

"Whoa! Yikes, looks like there is a giant fire over there." Char gazed out across the railroad tracks to the top of the tree line by the railroad tracks.

A siren rang out from behind us, and we could see it came from a cop car, headed toward us, zooming across the rickety bridge. The car almost caught some air when it shot off the steep incline onto the road. It raced along the gravel road toward the tracks and darted up the hill to the smoke.

I unhooked my leather pouch, threw it in the grass, and turned to Char. "Why don't you go grab our lunch bag and water? I lost my pouch in the tumble. I'll find it and meet you by the tree line."

"Sounds good." She took off toward the tracks.

Well, I took off too. By that I mean started moving. I watched her hike away. It still didn't look like she had her head on straight.

"You all right?!" I yelled.

"Yeah, I'll be okay," she reassured me, "feels like I am on a boat!"

I grabbed my pouch from the place where I'd thrown it, and peered down toward the river. A fresh stream of blood trickled down from the tree. Down the river, the dead man now only seemed to be a floating stump in the distance.

I caught up to Char, and we followed the bend of the railroad tracks.

"This must be what my dad feels like!" Char joked.

"Think so?" On the rare occasion that Char's dad was home, he was completely smashed, sloppy drunk.

"Yep. Got home from a trip yesterday. Don't know from where. But he went straight to the garage to spend some time with 'ol' Jack' as he says." She laughed. "My mum went out there to get him, probably because it was Mary's birthday."

"Mary? The dog?"

"Yea, we'll probably have a trip out to Maraine next weekend, for a little lake-side party. I'll let you know." Char continued, "Anyway, my Mom went out there and Dad started yellin' and screamin' like he does. I don't get why he comes back from those trucking ventures. Probably just doesn't have anywhere else to go."

I didn't have anything to say.

"You're lucky you've got such a good family."

I didn't look at her.

"Your dad gets mad, but he doesn't hit you. Mine hates me. Son-of-a-bitch."

I jerked my face around, and my eyes met her eyes. That was the first time I'd ever heard Char swear. I didn't know her mild-tempered soul was capable of cursing. But I guessed it had to come out sometime—all that fire running in her blood, but not from both sides of her family, fortunately. I think being a child of her mother, who was practically a saint, really saved her from being completely all bad. I thought of her as mixed breed, bad and good all at once. I think that is why I really took a liking to her back when we were little kids.

Flakes of ash trickled down through the sky onto our heads and shoulders, and we looked up. The overhead blue morning-light had grayed out. That smoke made the wind's pace visible. We walked through the dusty, sulfuric snow. And it slowly became clear that the fire was engulfing Covert's log cabin.

By the time we'd trekked down the tracks far enough to see it, the whole place had melted down to a pile of rubble. Firemen and EMTs were treading through blackened remains, flipping over and pushing around big pieces of nothing. One man tipped something backward, something that looked like it, about an hour earlier, was probably a refrigerator.

A baby-blue VW pulled up behind the house. A woman threw open the passenger's side door before the car was even stopped all the way. The driver, an old man, rushed out of the car, and followed the woman down the incline.

With both hands grasping her neck, she fell forward onto her knees. The old man lurched onto the ground next to her and pulled her into his embrace. I looked back down at the tracks.

Blood splattered the back of my eyes and the gurgling chokes of suffocation echoed around the inside of my skull. Using my periphery, I looked over at Char. She was also staring at the tracks, lunch bag in one hand and fist in the other. I could hear the large lumps of saliva forcing their way down my throat.

One of the police officers trampled down the steep incline toward the tracks.

I thought, oh good God, don't let him be coming to talk to us.

Stepping over branches and using the base of trees to ease his way, he landed at the foot of the train tracks and looked up to us. Char took her dead-pan stare from the tracks and glanced over at him with that gentle-sad smile that marks her face ninety-percent of the time.

"Good-a afternoon girls" he said. Deleone was the New Castle Police Chief. He and his wife also owned the bakery across from Popi's shoe shop.

Char answered, "Hello, sir."

I continued fighting off the chaos in my brain and attempted to look calm.

"My name-a is Chief Deleone," he continued, leaving no room for response. "What are you two young ladies doing down here?" He tried to suppress he slight Italian accent.

Again, Char answered, being the more congenial of the two of us. "We just finished looking around for some arrowheads down the tracks."

Officer Deleone's wide, rust-colored eyes looked alive and protruding against his dark olive skin. Raven black hair swirled out from under his cap. His bushy eyebrows caught various shapes of ash particles, including one that looked possibly like it could be smoldering still. A shiver shot down my spine.

"And how was-a your hunt?" Deleone asked Char.

"Oh, pretty decent. We found three in three hours," she responded. She paused for a moment. "What happened up at this house?"

"A fire, pretty quick one—in the last hou-," he clearly stopped short, even inappropriately ending the word "hour." "Did you two come down the tracks when you were going out to the field?"

My body shook. I surveyed his fresh, buttoned jacket, black pressed pants, and his shiny and yet dirt-drenched, black shoes. I rested my hand against my leather pouch. I could feel the corner of the photograph poking through the bottom seam. My mind raced. You're supposed to turn in the bad guys. They're supposed to get punished. Grandma, Bonanza, Mrs. Morganson, Jesus—what they all taught me.

"Yes, we did. We even saw this house and talked about . . . who was it, Rosie?" Char looked at me.

I disjointedly responded, kind of unsure of what Char even asked me, "Oh. Yeah. Mr. Covert's place right?"

Deleone's eyes pressed in on mine and then moved to Charlotte and then moved back to me. "Did you notice anything suspicious here?"

"No, sir. Nothing suspicious at all." Char answered for us.

Deleone's eyes shifted back to me. "How 'bout you?" I could see the tiny muscles beneath Deleone's right eye, pulsing. The same thing happens to Grandma when she tries to read a recipe card without her glasses.

When I looked into those dark eyes, fear shot through my bones.

"Anything out of the ordinary?" he asked.

"Umm." I had the photo. I had the proof. My mind darted back and forth. I'm supposed, supposed to turn him in right now, I thought.

I didn't know the full ramifications of what I was about to do when I did it. I was too young. My mind told me to do one thing, but my heart told me to do another. To this day I still vividly remember that ache under my ribs—that intuitive sense.

"No," I said. "Didn't see anything, either."

That answer, that lie, that clear deliberate honorable lie, changed everything.

Deleone peered at me. I couldn't keep my eyes focused on his.

"Okay. Now-a where exactly you search for arrowheads?"

He knew. I knew he knew I lied. He could see my damned soul.

"We were down in the field just past the curve," Charlotte turned and pointed down toward Covert's crossing. "Been there all morning until we heard the sirens," she finished.

"You two-a didn't hear or see anything odd? Would sure help with the investigation."

"No, not till the sirens, I guess." Charlotte shook her head.

"How did you get this lump on your forehead?" he asked. I hadn't noticed, but the goose-egg actually stuck out at least three-quarters of an inch.

"Oh, just tripped on the stairs this morning." Charlotte cheerily lied and even giggled a little.

Involuntarily, my head, snapped over to Char. Char never lied. Like, I had never heard her lie. That was the first time.

Deleone looked at Char and then looked at me. A lump was pulling all of my stomach and back muscles to a center, and my throat drained all the saliva producing the burning, scratchy feeling one gets when enduring a scary movie suspense scene. I wasn't even sure I could get out a word if I tried. So I didn't try. I just looked at him.

Deleone moved his gaze off into the distance then back up to the burn site. "Well, you girls better get'on home," Deleone ended the conversation. "Sorry for disturbing your trek. Thank you for answering these-a questions for me." Deleone smiled.

"You're welcome, sir." Char nodded. "No problem for us."

Deleone smiled, gave me a rusty-eyed wink, and continued back up to the cabin.

We walked few steps and then heard Deleone yell. "I almost forgot." He sounded excessively friendly. "Ladies, what are your names?"

"I'm Charlotte Pasicka and this is Rosemary Luce."

I didn't know why Char lied about the goose-egg. And I didn't intend to ask. Char's pretty bright and pretty trustworthy, but I guess she's just used to lying about that kind of stuff. I knew her dad hit all them—sloppy drunk bastard. I knew that some things you don't ask about. You just accept them.

We kept on our way back to Mahoningtown. My heart was in a weird kind of dull, trance-like state. I watched my legs walk. It seemed like my limbs moved in slow motion over the gravel. Everything looked so vivid. The trees were so vibrant, and every leaf seemed to speak out for itself. The strokes of wind brushed my face and weaseled through the curls that didn't quite make it into my ponytail. The smell of both ash and field stuck to the inside of my nose. I couldn't escape. Then, all at once, the world just seemed to rush at me. All at once.

When I regained consciousness, Char had me laying in the grass. "Looks like we are destined to the same fate my friend."

I sat up—my head spinning.

We laughed.

When Charlotte left me, I turned away from my house and rode the Line by myself.

When I returned home, pans clattered against each other and garlic puffed through the downstairs—no vampire would every dream of swooping in. Angelo, however, did swoop down the stairs. I slid straight against the wall as soon as I saw him. Before I knew it, he slipped right out the door, dropping a "Hey, Rose," point three seconds before the screen door's bombastic thunder.

My heart beat fast. Grandma clanged a pot. The sound struck my ears like lightning. It hurt so bad that my whole head thumped.

Ang swooped down the stairs like that all the time. I alternated squeezing shut one eye and then the other as I walked through the living room. Sliding into Grandma's rocking chair felt like a tree hugged you. I picked up Popi's newspapers and decided to have a read.

"Rosie!" Grandma called from the kitchen.

"Coming!" I set down the *New Castle News,* remembering my spot just above the coffee cup ring.

"You-a get-a-me some cheese?"

"Yep" I said. Damn, I thought. I hated descending into that slimy, dank basement. No matter how many times in my life I went down there, every time I came to terms that that was the time when someone would emerge from one of the dark corners and carry me off through a secret tunnel in the wall into a candle-lit chamber twanging with ghastly harpsichord dissonance.

Below the upper staircase I opened the door and started my way down the creaky wood planks. Every step had something to say. Some warned me. My only comfort was that I had a knife in my hand.

I slipped down the last few stairs and walked beside a long slice of light shining along the floor. Some cured meat and cheese hung from the ceiling with a stack of last year's wine piled under them. I lifted my knife to the cheese and cut off a wedge. As I made my way back to the stairs, a glistening jar of beets caught my eye. If this trip was going to momentarily rob me of my own sanity, I concluded, I might as well grab some contraband. Knife and cheese in one hand, contraband beets in the other, I started back up to the kitchen. The stairs still let out their cries, and I expected a devilish-green hand, with sharp gangly nails and tufts of dark hair to emerge from the darkness between the steps and grab hold of my ankle. My only choice was to pretend as though there was nothing there and that I was a normal person making a normal unworried trip up the basement stairs. I paused. I stepped up, my eyes on the lighted doorway.

I laid the cheese and beets on the table in the kitchen. Grandma still had her back to me as she continued her work at the stove. Leaving her to her own assumptions I made a quick exit so that I didn't have to explain the beets. While merrily strolling across the hall my sneaking success donned me with a rather foxy confidence.

"You help-a me roll-a meatball," Grandma stated. She didn't really have variation of any intonation when she spoke. It was always the same pattern—middle range start, peak at the second or third syllable, and then a steep slope down to the period, or comma, or whatever.

Rolling meatballs. The source of my demise, my arch-nemesis, my very own kryptonite—raw meat. I hated most that first plunge your hands must make into the cool, damp substance. Your hands start out warm and dry, which makes plunging into the depths of that slimy-with-eggs goo most horrifying. But, as it turns out, the more meatballs you roll, the more your mind forgets what you are actually doing, and the meat kind of becomes one with your body. Usually though, at that point you end up needing to scratch the itch on your neck or tuck your hair behind your ear, and then all of what you're doing ends up at the forefront of your brain again. You remember that you are basically shoving your hands into the side of a cow. You remember that that thing was actually once mooing and roaming a field, and that you might have perhaps even seen that cow, or even shot that cow with a water gun from the backseat window of your brother's car. It was after one of the itch moments that I returned my hands back to kneading and rolling.

Grandma put on the Nat Cole album. Nat's velvet voice followed Grandma into the kitchen. She and I sat there and rolled together.

Grandma was seriously in love with Nat Cole. I don't really know if she could even understand what he was singing, since she was hard of hearing and had to listen real hard to English syllables to make them out anyhow. Then she had to take the time to identify the words and syntax, tone and such. And she had to do that when people were just plain-old talking, not even singing. Nevertheless, she really loved his voice, and so did I. His words echoed through our rooms more than everyone else's words combined. Nat had become just a member of the family for us, and I grew used to his voice over the years, always there humming through the walls. When he wasn't singing, it seemed like something went missing.

The afternoon sun beamed down through the kitchen window. Our shadows were cast onto that dastardly, yet tender, formica table top. Stark silhouettes of hands and arms and fingers danced about, and heads swayed back and forth. I hadn't noticed my shoulder muscles were all tight and hovering next to my ears. They unfurled under Nat's hypnotic voice. Grandma's face-skin kind of glistened. A little ridge of sweat gathered at her upper lip and twinkled in the warm light. I was sure our hands were sucking up a pungent garlic scent. I heard that if you eat too much garlic, you start to smell like it. I didn't much understand why that was a bad thing.

I didn't mind the glaring moonbeam bearing down on my eyes. I hadn't slept for the first four hours of the night, so why would I sleep for the last four? No moonbeam could interfere with my night. I wouldn't let it. Popi and Dad had put the news on after dinner. I didn't stay to watch, but Popi's hearing was so bad by that point that he had to keep the volume on the "outrageously loud" setting. I could hear it. A report on the Covert fire interrupted the nightly round of tri-county goings-on. The newscaster's voice was stark and metallic when he rolled out the details—electrical fire, investigation, 1 p.m., Covert likely trapped in the house, trapped, trapped, trapped.

Under that moonbeam, my mind accommodated a chalkboard with no chalk, utterly blank and incapable of undoing the blankness. And that's the state I had been in for the past four hours. The crucifix slid down my chest and loped over my shoulder onto the bed. I stared up at the crack shaped like the Eastern seaboard that ran along my ceiling. Everything in me fought to get away from that daytime nightmare. My eyes flowed over it, from top to bottom, over and over and over again. Maine. Massachusetts. Rhode Island. Connecticut. New York, New Jersey, Delaware, Maryland, Virginia, North Carolina. A surge of pain filled my abdomen, my eyes went glassy. I launched myself to the side of my bed and vomited into the trashcan. Then I rolled back over. South Carolina, Georgia, Florida.

The sky embraced the earth with a deep, dark shade of blue, and a lone bird sung out in the darkness. Dawn stewed, reluctant to emerge from its hiding place. The clouds rolled on in, tumbling slowly, threatening to conceal the high plain of the sky.

I could see Dad sitting out on the front porch. Still—silent. Gazing out on Elm Street. Generally, I never got up quite that early. But after a night of staring at the ceiling, I padded my way down the stairs as soon as it would be fitting. When I finished navigating where the squeaks hid on the stairs, I looked up. Yes, I looked up the hall before entering the kitchen. That's when I saw Dad reclined, cigarette in hand and an ever-lightening blue on the side of his face. It set my spirit at ease. Just being there with him, noticing him without him knowing. Seeing him just be without the demands of social responsibility. He looked down at something. I couldn't quite see, considering the distance as well as the slight haze built up on the lower corners of the window. I took a reprieve from my pursuit of coffee to just watch him a little while longer. I leaned up against the living room's pale door frame. My robe tie slunk down from my waist, so I haphazardly adjusted it. The daze of sleep lingered in my skin, and my motor skills were not exactly efficient.

Dad just sat there puffing smoke and reading something. He and Nicky sure did look alike from the back. Their thick dark hair and hard-working shoulders looked the same, but the real similarity was their common essence—the way they sat, a relaxed confidence that could easily be mistaken for arrogance, stroking the hair on the back of their heads while flicking their cigarette butts like ex-pat bar owners waiting for a plane of tourists to descend. It was a real father-son miracle.

I hadn't seen Dad too much in the past few months. He had taken some extra shifts down at the mill to finally pay off the hospital bill, outstanding since Mom left. In fact, he was usually off on his bicycle by that blue hour, on the way to the mill. I hoped he had the day off. He didn't.

I wished I knew him better. But he was just so quiet, and so was I. I thought he was a good man, though. From what I could tell, I knew that he loved us, but it was like he had twenty million things to say and for some reason he kept them all locked away. Or he feared saying them. Saying anything at all is pretty scary. I had no space to lament his silence. I knew it all too well then. My own secrets began to imprison me, and I wondered if Dad had seen such horrible sights too.

I've grown to see mouths as more or less replicas of our gigantic bay window. Strung-back lips reveal windows that lead directly to you, the real you, the you that you are not real sure that even you know. The worst part, I've found, is you never know how people will react. You can never really tell what will happen after you talk. Sometimes you take the time to open up that window to yourself's self and people don't even care.

He puffed another cloud and set down his cigarette hand on the arm of the chair. His right hand went up—head, chest, shoulder, shoulder. Perhaps it was horror that made him pray. The lingering smoke swirled around him like silk. After putting out the flame, he stood up and carried the book to the front door. I dashed into the kitchen, started filling up the kettle and tried to be as usual as possible. What an embarrassment it would be if my sentimentality was found out. I waited for the sound of the door. The water was on the stove, high heat. But the floorboards never creaked.

I peeked around the corner out of the kitchen. The front door remained silent at the end of the darkened hallway. A flicker of light bounced off the living room's far wall. I leapt in to see out the window. Dad's bicycle rim flicked more sunlight as he rode across the front of the house down Elm. For some time I feared that he was virtually unknowable. I wished I knew him, but I recognized I never would. I would have liked to know about why we all turned out the way we did. I thought perhaps understanding the strange imminent weight of the blood that flowed in my veins would be relieving, or maybe moreover consoling. If I would have talked to anybody about this it would have been Dad—cause I dreamed he'd listen unfazed and offer up some good simple reason and some healing remedy. Then he'd explode into a thousand words and tell me all about how he saw the world, and what he thought of each of us kids, and how he loved me, and why he prayed.

I dejectedly lumbered out the front door and onto the porch. The single bird's song had turned into that of four or five birds, and the sky lightened into periwinkle. The porch still smelled like cigarettes. An ember glowed in the ash tray. Beneath the smoke, though, lingered the scent of Dad—a very particular flavor that I have grown accustomed to, and fond of, over the many years of lying face down on his bed in the morning after he got up.

I strode toward the little wooden step-stool next to his chair. The ash-tray concealed under its rippled edges an unused cigarette. That particular cigarette had been there, for who knows how long, and I never saw Dad offer it to anyone. If one of the *ragazzi* came up to visit, Dad always pulled a fresh one out of his pack.

Several men cycled past, also on their way to the mill. You could pick the mill workers out easily because they all wore the same brushed-leather, steel-toed boots.

I ran my fingers along the chain that circled my neck. It felt so soft. Even the knobby crucifix was soft. I imagined the countless hands that had run over that very chain: one of them a nun, one of them a hoodlum, and probably all kinds of other people. I knew it was about that time, the time I ought to be turning over that crucifix. I decided that I didn't have to confess or repent or anything. It wasn't my fault that I stole; Hog forced me into it, and I thought it was okay in the moment. Honestly, when I swiped it, I really did think I was doing a good and noble thing.

I tossed my robe over a kitchen chair and grabbed my shoes before arriving at the front door. It didn't matter that I hadn't changed out of my pajamas, because I usually slept in real life clothes.

The streets were still quiet, save the sprinkling of cyclists. I could almost hear my own thoughts out loud. A light flashed on in Deleone's Bakery. When I passed it, I saw Mrs. Deleone wiping the windows. Her kind eyes lit up, and she waved. Behind her sat a man, Jimmy Mancini, one of Popi's best pals in those days. Jimmy drank his coffee at the same table every day. That's where I met him the previous summer, at that very table.

Popi and I had gone down to the bakery, not for any reason —really just to shoot the breeze and have a flaky pastry of some sort. I was complimenting Popi's English when we walked in. It was true, he'd started to improve quite a bit. I mean, really, it was a wonder how he got along all those years since the move from "the mother land." It took him like seventy years to get even adequate at the common tongue, probably due to the fact that he'd married an Italian, hung out with Italians, and settled in an Italian neighborhood. He was just rarely forced to speak English, which was not his fault. The only practice he got was when Polaks or Irish or Czecks or even Germans down from Wampum stopped in at his shoe shop for repair of the sole or new laces or a new heel, or whatever. It really wasn't until I came along that he spoke in English for any considerable amount of time— from what I understand. Dad told me that Grandma and Popi would send him off to school as an Italian-speaking six-year-old and then have him teach them when he got home. So that's how they learned enough to get by.

When Popi opened the door that day, we had both witnessed Mrs. Deleone putting out her world-famous cannoli. I don't much care for cannoli, but Popi was an addict. Jimmy Mancini's eyes darted over the newspaper that he held about six inches away from his thick-like-fishbowl-lensed glasses. Once Popi had ordered our delicacies and stole his coffee mug from the top of the pastry case Jimmy invited us to sit with him at the little round table by the front window— wouldn't have been my choice of seating, since that table and two out of three chairs rocked at least an inch at every slight movement. Nevertheless, there we docked, right before the mostly blind and curiously perceptive, great Mancini.

CHAPTER 9

Mancini, whom everyone called "the Pepper," definite article always included, and Popi, whom everyone called "Rooster," definite article never included, ended up getting on the subject of fruit trees. How they got there I don't know, seeing that I had spent the first ten minutes of the conversation keeping my face fairly peaceful and respectful, but seriously trying to negotiate with my own brain, which kept wrinkling up every time Jimmy Mancini rested his hand next to his coffee and clunked that godforsaken table back onto its window-side leg. That alone could drive an eleven-year-old girl out of her mind. I mean, come on. I was already dealing with the fact that my arms hung slightly longer than necessary for my body size, and also with my sudden fits of unintended rage. Alas, I decided to just imagine that we had all boarded one of those fancy ships that sailed down the coast to South America. The table was just shifting from the waves. By that point, Popi and the Pepper were on to the fruit tree conversation. Any conversation about fruit trees literally forced Popi into the story of his immigration from "the mother land."

Popi, then called "Raphael," celebrated his thirteenth year just before his parents sent him off with his twin brother, Alfonso, to the new world. In the year 1904, Raphael and Alfonso set off on their journey across the Atlantic with a nickel in each pocket. Nickels back then were worth more, but honestly, it still couldn't have amounted to much.

Apparently, these teens landed at a port in Florida with no English skills, four nickels, and the clothes on their backs. When the boat drifted to the dock, it got stuck. A four-and-a-half-meter gap separated the boat from the dock itself. Legend has it that Popi didn't know how to swim, but his brother Alfonso did. So while Alfonso, along with the other passengers, swam across, Popi walked. Yeah, that's what I said. Popi insisted that he walked across the ocean floor, having to bounce up to get a breath when he needed it. People believed him too. I don't know what kind of people did believe it, because I knew that even dead men float.

Popi said that after they got off the boat, they decided to have a look at a US map. And from that very map, Popi pointed out New Castle, Pennsylvania, and decided to move there. So they made their way from Florida two thousand miles up the coast to New Castle and settled down. They quickly were notified that all the Italians lived in either Mahoningtown, a land by the river with air filled with steel-smoke and train soot, or Hillsville, the truest Transylvania of modern existence. I imagined that Hillsville held a conglomeration of various national specimens, whipping out all their problems and therein calling upon a most serious witchcraft. Raphael chose Mahoningtown because he liked the city living. It reminded him of home.

Soon enough, Popi mysteriously got his hands on some equipment and set up his shoe shop, but as for Alfonso, he became discontented with the little town. So he moved up to Canada by hitching a ride with a man selling fruit trees. And so it came to pass that we have some Canadian-Italian relatives, which I found and find completely confusing.

By the time I finished mentally recounting that story inspired by seeing Jimmy "the Pepper" Mancini, I arrived at St. Mary's. By then the sun glared through cracks of clouds. I entered the church and touched the Holy Water. After stepping into the sanctuary, I slid into the back pew. Father Piccolo emerged from the foyer. It seemed like people always snuck up on me in that place, even when I sat in the back row.

I forced out some words. "Good Morning, Father Piccolo," I said, schooling my voice to give it a rather calm and carefree timbre.

"Good Morning, child," he replied. "What is your name?" His voice reminded me of salt and pepper. It was comforting and distinctive; it had a savory quality. The kind of voice that you would want to listen to for a few hours, but would end up falling asleep after the first fifteen minutes.

"I'm Rosemary Luce."

"Ah, yes, Luce." He nodded with his eyes shut. "Your grandfather owns the shoe shop?" Father Piccolo was still fairly new, so he didn't have all the details down yet.

"Yep, that's him."

"Well I am glad to see you here. I noticed you often come to pray in the morning." I wondered if he was patronizing or genuinely kind. "What brings you down?"

"Well." My eyes kind of dashed around, floor to ceiling, Mary to Jesus and back again. "I, uh," my words stumbled over each other so that it sounded like Scottish, "I come in . . . well, just to pray as usual, and . . ."

He doubted, I was sure of it. His eyebrows lifted, yet his forehead remained the same height given that, save a few hairs, his forehead was abnormally high for a man at his less-than-middle age.

"Well," I continued with staunch certainty, "I've come to confess."

Piccolo broke out into a booming laughter. The walls resonated, and the candle flames even caught vibrations.

I almost wet my pants it was so alarming. I didn't know you could laugh in the house of God. I thought maybe that was the first time the statues heard laughter since their sculptor's studio.

He folded his arms on top of his legs and stroked one elbow as he considered something. Just then a few women trickled into the church bearing pots of flowers.

"Good morning, Father Piccolo." The solemn-sounding greeting came from a woman with curly, triangle-shaped hair carrying mums.

He looked up to her and nodded. "Good morning, Teresa. Let me know if there's anything I can do to help as you prepare."

"We'll let you know. Thank you."

Suddenly, to my surprise and dismay, Mrs. Pasicka walked through the doorway. There was no way I could escape now.

And of course she immediately recognized me. "Oh, Rosie! Good to see you. You ought to come up to the house. Haven't seen you in ages."

I rolled my eyes up to meet hers. "Yeah. Yeah, I was thinkin' that too."

She moved her hand down and lovingly rubbed my shoulder blade. I prayed to God that she wouldn't see that chain around my neck.

"Father, the prayer meeting? Should we postpone until after the funeral?"

He nodded and his face bore a somber expression. "I think that would be wise."

"I'll let the others know."

A silence loomed.

Mrs. Pasicka looked down to me. "Rosie, you should come to our prayer meeting. You'd be the youngest, but there is another young lady. She's in high school. I think she goes to New Castle." Her quizzical eye moved to Father Piccolo for confirmation.

"Yes," he concurred, "I believe that's true."

Everybody always looked to the priests for certainty. I guess people who heard confession had all the low-down on society, what was true and not. I didn't know him well enough to believe that, though.

Mrs. Pasicka looked back at me. "We'll meet here tomorrow evening then? Perhaps the same time, around seven or so. "

Time was fluid in those parts. Her hand rested on my shoulder for I don't know how long.

I can't, I just can't, I thought. I can't do this now. I can't confess, I told myself. With great certainty I knew that they'd think me to be a thief. I'm not a thief, I come from a good family. We Luces are good, honest people. We're good and honest. That's right. Good and honest. And I can't let people think different.

"Rosie?" Piccolo leaned forward to look at my face. "What do you think about that?"

I had no idea what they were talking about now. I agreed anyway. "Oh, yeah. It's okay."

"Oh, Rosie," Mrs. Pasicka burst out. She patted me on the shoulder. "Come up and visit soon, alright?"

I nodded.

"Oh, and we are having a fishing day at Maraine. Charlotte probably told you that though, right?"

"Yep. Mary's birthday."

Mrs. Pasicka smiled. "There are many reasons to celebrate. We just have to find them!"

The woman with the triangular hair, plant still in hand, slid into the pew before us. "Father, we were wondering . . . "

That was my cue, I jumped up, exited the church, and pranced down the cement stairs. Parked on the street was a baby-blue VW. At the sight of it I sucked in a big breath of air. As I passed it, I peered into the back windows to see if I could identify anyone who might be inside. But I couldn't really see anything because of the sun's reflection.

Across the street two intense men speedily walking around the corner and passed the CCD building. Their strides elongated with every step, and their speed accelerated. Pretty soon they both were in full-out sprint. Sirens rang out in the distance—my guess, a trail of cop cars spinning down

Jefferson Hill. I watched as the two men closed in on the parish house. The priests used to live there, but Father Piccolo never moved in. Instead he had turned it into a half-way house. Those two *ragazzi* slid under the front porch. Just before the cop cars swirled around the corner the men had vanished from sight.

Unfazed, I looked back at the VW. Was it theirs? I didn't hang around to find out. Instead, I wheeled back around and took off to Mahoningtown.

That VW was the car at the scene of the fire. And upon seeing it, something really did stir in me. Something knotted in my stomach and told me that things were not what they seemed. Meanwhile a little bird landed on my shoulder as I jogged home. He asked me, "What are you going to do about this?"

"I don't know, I mean, what is there for me to do?"

"You know what you saw out there."

"A man got slit up! That's all I know," I puffed out with irregular jog-ging-type breath.

"What does it mean?" the bird tweeted. "Come on, Rosie, what does it mean?"

"What do *you* mean? You dumb bird!"

"What should you do about this?"

"Nothing. It's just life. Bad things happen. I can't do anything about it."

I took off, accelerating to a full out sprint. But just when I sped into the alley behind Cascade Street, my shoelace unraveled. When I slipped across some loose stones, I stepped on that lace, tried to stop myself, but fell to a screeching halt on one knee.

The ground peeled the flesh right off my knee cap. A little flap of skin still hung there. I ripped the dangling skin off and bubbles of blood rose to the surface. I wiped them off and stood up. My knee felt like somebody had breathed on it with either fiery or icy breath. But fear of what I knew drove me faster than the pain could stop me. So after walking a few steps, I broke back into my jog. Wiping the trickling blood was the least of my worries. As I rounded the corner by Hyde's Drug Store, my temples pounded due to the pressure caused by my clenched teeth.

Carmine was out sweeping his front step. A sour taste welled up in my mouth. As I passed him, I looked away, pretending to look at something interesting in the distance. But my eyes swelled with tears, so much so that I couldn't see anything, let alone something interesting in the distance.

I hadn't retied my shoe. Both laces swung wildly when I leapt onto the sidewalk at Elm Street. My feet raced to avoid them. Once Carmine was fully behind me and I was away from the threat of having to speak to a live human, my jog slowed to a walk. I wiped the wetness away from my eyes. Giving my cheeks a little pat, I pulled myself together.

Grandma was probably awake and in the kitchen making some coffee for herself—decaf of course. I wasn't ready to watch her look into my scared eyes. I feared what she'd say when she looked into my accursed eyes. Just after I stepped up onto the porch, Nicky swung open the screen door. His glare struck me back, nailing me into the open space behind me.

"Are you dumb, Rosie?" He screamed as he grabbed me by the shirt collar. "You *gidrul*!"

I wondered for which crime he was accusing me. What did he know? "What?" I trembled under his grip. "I . . . I . . . " I reached up to feel the crucifix, wondering if it had given me away. No girl I ever seen wore a chain. We all had rosaries, but nobody actually wore them around their necks—except nuns of course, and I wasn't any holy sister. But it lay safely beneath my shirt.

"You left the burner on!" His arm veins bubbled up as his grip tightened.

"I . . . I . . . "

"What, Rosie?! What kind'a stupid excuse you gonna make now?"

Tears streamed down my face, "I didn't know . . . I . . . I forgot."

"You FOR-GOT, oh, of course little Rosie just forgot again." He sneered.

All of the rage that had been piling up in me released itself into my bones. My arms swung wildly and bashed Nicky anywhere they could manage. He snagged both of my wrists and I tried to shake him off. "Let go of me, you bastard!"

Nicky released his hands and landed a southpaw punch right on the side of my face. I fell onto my side in front of Dad's chair and for a second I couldn't figure out which way was up. It took less than a second for my face to feel stung like a giant wasp got me and for my mouth to fill with a thick, salty liquid. I wiped away the saliva running down my chin.

Angelo barreled out the door, tackling Nicky from behind. Through blurry vision I could see Nicky's arms were skinned by the gnarly wooded porch. I placed my spit-drenched hand on the ground to support me, and that's when I saw the blood. I spit out the excess of liquid in my mouth and blood spattered the legs of the chair. The world spun around and I tried to make it stable again.

"Are you out of your mind?" Nicky yelled as he struggled to flip Angelo off him.

"ME?" Angelo screamed back. "You're the damned bastard . . . "—punched Nicky in the face—" . . . that hit my sister!"

Nicky in one motion threw Angelo off to his side and pinned one of his arms to the ground. "She could'a got us killed!"

Angelo swung his loose arm at Nicky, but Nicky caught it mid-swing. "We could'a died in our sleep," Nicky seriously whispered. "All of us." His head slowly moved toward Angelo's head. He wrested his forehead on Angelo's forehead. "I don't want us to be the next Covert." Nicky's voice smoothed out, and Angelo's breathing slowed.

Angelo looked down and shook his wrists free from Nicky's loosening grip. He pushed Nicky back onto his side and leapt over to me.

At that point, I sat cross-legged on the porch watching, just letting blood run down my chin and drip onto the wood between my legs. Angelo put his hand on the sides of my head and pulled my face up to his eyes. He started fiddling around with my face, hinging my jaw open and looking inside. He was just kind of a ghost to me, a moving figure in undefined proximity. I could hear my heart beating in my throat and ears—soft and constant. Its lullaby lured me to sleep, but Angelo kept pulling my eyelids back open and telling me to stay awake.

CHAPTER 10

Carmine Carmidio came run-hobbling to the stairs, probably alarmed by the screaming.

Angelo turned to him. "Mr. Carmidio, thank God," he said. "I think she has a concussion, and she's torn up real bad in the mouth." He grabbed hold of my lower lip. "Especially on the lip here."

Carmine stepped up onto the porch and took a knee beside Angelo. He looked into my eyes and inspected my face and head. I could see Nicky behind him laying on the ground. He was facing me, one eye-white covered in blood. The skin around his eye was puffed out and pale. He just collapsed there on his side looking at me, his face all drooped, and his body, completely silent. He just looked at me like that.

Carmine picked me up and carried me down the stairs. "I'm taking Rosie over to my store to get fixed up," he said. Then he added, "You boys better get all this straightened out real quick." Carmine glared at them, "You hear me?"

"Yes" Angelo said, obedience in his voice.

"Yes, sir." Nicky's words sounded more like a groan.

Carmine walked me over to his store with one of my arms slung around his neck. When we got inside, he sat me up on the counter and fished through a couple of drawers.

"Where're Grandma and Popi?" I asked.

"Just left before you got here," Carmine quickly answered, signaling he had something else, something mort important on his mind. He was still focused on his drawer-rifling. But his voice softened. "Walked down to St. Mary's I'd assume. Funeral." He stuffed some gauze into my mouth, filling out my left cheek. After that, he got to work on my lip.

"Why didn't you go down to the funeral?" I asked.

He didn't answer. He continued staring intently at the damage done. Whatever his reason, I was glad he did stay back.

My eyes swung around, observing the store. The world had regained its stability, and all the colors were back to their normal hues again. My shoulders had relaxed, and my body felt at peace sitting there motionless atop the counter. Suddenly, I felt a certain lightness where a heaviness had been. Literally. I slapped my hand over my chest—no crucifix.

"Okay." Carmine stepped back and handed me a little bottle of liquid from the counter. "Here. Take this into the bathroom and swish out your mouth for about ten seconds—sing "Happy Birthday" in your head."

I hoped off the counter and strode to the bathroom at the far end of the store. I told myself the crucifix must have fallen off somewhere, and sucked in a big swig of the anonymous liquid. That stuff was hotter than a spoonful of hell-fire and damnation. I whipped it around my mouth and the lightning of judgment struck every crack in my broken flesh. Spitting it out into the sink was the greatest mercy. Though I didn't even make it through, "and many, many more."

Carmine said I could go home. So I thanked him and exited through the front door. Suddenly a memory slapped me in the face. So instead of going straight home, I turned around the backside of Hyde's. I remembered having a significant impression that my crucifix slipped off when I tripped. Lo and behold, a shimmer lay in the distant gray gravel. I examined the chain and found it had split near the clasp. After a bout of dismay, I determined that the break was an easy fix with a safety pin.

I put the crucifix in the pocket of my shorts, and it weighed them down. My clothes kind of hung on me, anyway. I always hated wearing the same clothes for too long. They started to feel recognizable, like when you notice that you're wearing something instead of just wearing it. I had one of those recognizable feelings just then.

I stepped out of the alley to head toward home. A woman with thick, raven hair and a woman wearing a long-sleeve, long-skirted black dress muttered on the stairs of a front porch. Their eye-darting close-talking put me at a great unease, yet—as my mind still withheld strands innocent stupidity—a greater intrigue. When I made it to the sidewalk of Cascade, also I noticed a group of men several blocks down. They huddled, almost in our yard, on the corner of Elm and Cascade, stealing glances first at the house and then at me. Their discussion seemed to be one big, tame whisper.

Instead of trampling in through the back door, which I felt sure was locked anyway, I tracked through the grass over to the front. I did my best to keep from making eye contact with the men, but I strained my ears to pull out any of their words. I couldn't make out one.

Grandma's tough, muscular hands were whacking a scrub brush hard against the porch wood.

Next to her sat a bucket of soapy water. I could see that her apron was damp from being dragged across the wet porch. She knelt there, scrubbing away. So I knelt on the other side of her and scrubbed, in my own way. Spatters of blood dotted the surface before me. Mine? Nicky's? Angelo's? It all looked the same.

Grandma was quiet that day. I can see why, though. She and Popi had risen early to walk down to St. Mary's for Covert's funeral. Then they arrived home, doubtless ready to change out of their black, when they found blood stains of their own kin sprayed across the front porch.

Angelo gone. Me gone. Nicky inside lying on the couch with a bag of frozen peas on his face. Grandma always had something to be joyful about; she found something funny or fun in every situation.

Some tear drops splashed onto the porch. I didn't ask about her tears. She didn't ask about my face. The world was gray, and we scrubbed. She didn't even look at me, but I'm glad she didn't, because I could still feel the swelling in my face.

I finished with my section and sat there, staring out on the empty Elm street. A couple of cars meandered by, bringing with them a bite-sized breeze. I figured Grandma must have finished too. She scooted around to the stairs and placed her feet on the steps. The moment was kind of nice. Not enjoyable, but nice, just being under the gray skies with her.

The men on the corner had dispersed while we were scrubbing, but the street still resonated with a kind of quiet chaos. I don't know if Grandma noticed.

Later that day, I had plopped into Grandma's cherry-wood rocking chair. Popi had it specially made by some woodworking *dagos* out in Hillsville.

I nestled in and popped a dark, tart cherry into my mouth. When I spit the seed in the ash tray, a muddled thud dunged. The newspaper rested on my crossed leg. I popped another cherry in; my eyes scanned the sports column looking for Angelo's name.

Angelo had fought a few boxing matches that past week up in Mercer. As usual, I had asked about them last Sunday, and so he told me a couple of stories about some guy that spit on him from over a balcony and how his slobber moved in slow-motion until it slung over his right foot. That's all he said. Because Angelo just plain wouldn't talk about himself, I was left, weekly, to search the papers to find out just how badly he beat everyone. Unfortunately, Popi had left the papers strewn out of order.

A sizzling sound emerged from the kitchen. Meatballs had hit the frying pan once and again—making a kind of collective sizzle that grew with every sphere Grandma added. I spit out four seeds and turned the page. The picture on A-1, which I pulled from the middle of the stack, was of the Covert cabin, or what was formerly the Covert cabin. I could smell the smoke. Just below the photograph stood "Richard Charles Covert" wearing his US Army suit. And the headline said, "Man Presumed Dead after Fire." I read the story:

Yesterday afternoon the home of Richard Charles Covert was found extinguished by what has now been proven to be an electrical fire. Residents of Mahoningtown, three miles east of Covert reported seeing smoke blowing in from the area mid-morning. But, it wasn't until 1 PM that authorities arrived on the scene after receiving a call from a man scavenging in the nearby woods. The witness, Nicholas Raphael Luce . . .

My heart stopped. I shut the paper and peered around the corner into the kitchen. Grandma's floral dress whipped out from behind the door frame and back behind it again. I opened the paper again.

The witness, Nicholas Raphael Luce, reported to the police from the Hyde's Drug Store phone, 12:30 PM. He reported hearing a man's screams, which led him to the house. By the time he arrived, at approximately 11:30 AM, however, the structure was covered in flames. The whereabouts of its occupant, Richard Charles Covert, are presently unclear. The authorities have presumed that Covert was trapped in his house, but his body has not been recovered.

Oddly enough, Popi's coffee-cup stain was not on that page. Therefore, I deduced, it was likely I was the only person in this house who knew about Nicky's involvement in the Covert story.

The front door creaked a long hiss, and the screen door slammed shut. Charlotte's aunt and uncle had a screen door that magically shuts, slowly and evenly with no clatter. Honestly, I didn't mind the clatter too much. It was kind of like having a door bell. But it is a pain to worry about getting a chunk of your heel taken off by the machete-like bottom edge.

The cause of the slam was definitely Angelo. He had a way of flinging the door open so the hinges nearly ripped off the frame and then hopping in to avoid the machete. The sound of this maneuver distinguished him from any other door opener. As I listened to the sound of his steps, slow and pensive, I shut the paper and picked up the bowl of cherries. Angelo came lumbering down the hallway. As he passed into the door way I could see that he was looking through the mail.

I might as well start this conversation, I thought, before he gets the chance to ask me what I am doing in here. I didn't want to have to make up some kind of response right on the spot. "Anything good in there?" I yelled from the rocking chair.

Angelo, eye's still down, replied, "Nope, nothing," and threw the stack of envelopes onto the end table by the couch. He turned to the bobbing record player and flipped Nat Cole to side A before proceeding up the stairs.

I waited until Angelo reached the top step, before I put the bowl of cherries back on the coffee table and flipped open the newspaper again. The picture of the Covert house was somehow alluring as is retelling a nightmare. A knot formed in my stomach, and my mouth got all that dryness stuck in it, but, I just kept on looking. The house was gone. He was gone. The little VW was off to the corner of the picture. I figured the photo must have been taken after Charlotte and I had passed. A woman's shoe tilted up against a tree on the right perimeter of the shot. It was a dark-colored high-heel. It, perhaps, belonged to the woman who stumbled out of the VW onto the ground. Her shrieks cut through my memory. Suddenly, I was there again. I was watching the beaten man being dragged through the tall grasses.

Pound-pound. Pound-pound. My heart thudded up against my lungs.

I was back in the field heaving that giant rock. "Help me, Rosie! Help me," the corpse called. Maggots crawled out over my hands and up my arms. Then the woman's shrieks were there, and suddenly they filled my own lungs. The screams dug their nails in my throat. And I realized the shrill, painful screaming woman had escaped from my own mouth, completely drowning out Nat's Mona Lisa.

Poor Grandma! She lurched through the kitchen door, her eyes bugging out and her hair disheveled. At the same time, Angelo came bounding down the stairs. Three steps and he was down the whole flight. At roughly the same instant they both zoomed into the living room.

Grandma rushed at me. "Rosie!"

"Rosie, what happened?! You alright?" Angelo breathlessly puffed out.

The newspaper had already floated down covering my socked feet. But my hands were still extended, as if still holding the invisible news.

"Rosie! What happened?" Angelo shouted.

Grandma sat on the coffee table directly in front of me, her hands stroking my shoulders. Grandma and Ang were just figures, blurry figures. I fought to bring them into view and they slowly morphed into actual three-dimensional people before me. My hands lowered to my thighs. "I . . ." I didn't know what to say.

Grandma looked into my eyes, "You imagine something girl?"

"Yes, yes." I took what seemed to be like a cue from her. "I just scared myself."

Angelo patted my head. "I knew she shouldn't have watched Frankenstein," he muttered into his cheek.

Which, I couldn't argue with. I actually should not have gone to see Frankenstein the previous week. "I'm okay. It's okay." I tried my best to assure them with a grin.

"You sure?" Grandma asked.

I nodded. "I'm good now." I could feel the pink embarrassment rising on my face.

Nat sang in the corner.

"Why don't you come help-a me roll meat-a-balls in-kitchen?" Grandma gently shook my shoulder, "Huh?"

I began to rise. "Think I will."

Angelo gave me a couple pats on the head and retreated back up to his perch.

Grandma slowly stood up from the table, unhinging her rusty knees, "We-a gonna have fun."

Both of us stood. Her arm extended around my back and squeezed me into her well-padded side. We walked into the kitchen. She pulled out a seat for me at that ugly, tarnished, yellowy, laminate-topped table.

By the time I rolled three meatballs, it seemed my strange scream in the living room had happened in a year past. It kind of felt like I had become another person entirely, or inhabited a dream or something and now was visited by some ghost. It occurred to me that the New Castle Newspaper was still lying on the floor. Nobody even asked about it or looked at it, from what I can remember. I was glad.

"I'm goin' to the bathroom." I turned to Grandma. "Be right back." I scooted the chair back and leapt out of the kitchen. On my way to the toilet, I peeked back into the living room. The paper was of course still there on the floor—Covert house face up. I looked back over my shoulder, and seeing Grandma busy at the stove, I tip-toe-pranced back into the living room and snatched up that single front page. After I tip-toe-pranced back out, I passed the kitchen and stairs and headed toward the bathroom. I was careful not to look at the picture while I folded it up. From my position seated on the toilet, I had to stretch to reach the cupboard beneath the sink.

In the back of the cupboard I previously formed a collection of toilet paper rolls. When I fully extended my arm, my finger tips brushed up one of the ends. I sat back and re-centered myself and extended out again. This time my index and middle finger clamped down on one of them. I pulled it out from its position. One renegade roll leaped out onto the floor, but luckily nothing else fell out of place. After folding up the newspaper page into a very tight, near equilateral square. I wedged it into the safety of the toilet paper roll and set the cylinder on the floor.

When I finished my toilet ritual, I placed the roll beneath the others all the way in the back corner, and I tossed the renegade from the floor back into the cupboard. I washed my hands, careful to get the newsprint off, and headed out to resume my meatball duties. But the thought sprung to mind that I hadn't washed my hands before handling the paper. And so now I had a mangled newspaper page drenched in meaty bacteria festering in an empty toilet paper roll beneath the downstairs bathroom sink. Even stranger though, this seemed to me to be, like, quite an appropriate place for it.

"Rosie!" Grandma called from the kitchen. "You get-a me whipped cream."

She was totally inthralled by that new innovation in whipped cream technology, yet she didn't keep whipped cream in the house. I'm assuming she either feared that Popi or Dad might see and start complaining that it "didn't taste as good." So, repetitively, she dragged me into the job. I strode into the kitchen, snatched the change from her hand, and proceeded toward the door. "Need anything else?"

"No. *Grazie!*"

I was happy to get out of there. I knew that Dad would be coming home from work in the next few minutes, and Grandma would tell him all about our brawl on the front porch. I never got yelled at, that was a perk of being the youngest and the girl. So I knew he wouldn't raise his voice at me, but he would see my face. When we got into something, the fault usually landed on Angelo, since I was a girl and Nicky was the favorite. But this time would be different, because it was obvious that Nicky laid the punch on me. Who knew what might happen if Nicky decided to lie and say that Ang was the one who struck first.

I left the house, locked the door, and dashed across the street to Hyde's. I always did find it odd that drug stores were so inclusive about random products. Ninety-eight percent of the time, I was sent there for a random baking necessity—not drugs. I peered down Cascade and up Elm. The streets still empty, even the wind had left them.

The big green door at Hyde's weighed against me. I pushed it open and entered the beloved neighborhood drug store. The bell dinged, but no Carmine. I went down the aisle with the baked goods toward the couple of refrigerators that buzzed in the back corner. The bell gave an alarm. Someone else had come through the door. I figured it was Carmine, so I quickly spun around on the heel of my saddle shoe. It wasn't.

Instead, it was two men, and Carmine was nowhere in sight.

The two men stood in the doorway. The taller one reached up and ripped the bell right off of the door frame and threw it. The heavy metal crashed against the cement wall.

The shorter guy walked up to the counter. "Carmine!" He yelled a yell of sandpaper mixed with thick spit.

I slid down to my knees and then onto my stomach. Below the horizon of Wonderbreads, I could see the taller one scuffling at the door, and from the sound, locking it. They hadn't seen me, and I planned to keep it that way. My heart thumped against the crucifix.

"Carmine, get your ass down here *struppiau!*" The man at the counter pounded his fist. "SON-OF-A-BITCH!" He picked up one of the candy jars and slammed it on the ground. It shattered. The Tootsie Rolls scattered out onto the floor. One particular Tootsie slid under three rows of products and hit my trembling hands. I let my legs slide out from under me until I lay flat on the floor. Footsteps clunked, invisible, in the middle of the wall behind me. After descending the stairs, Carmine came out from the doorway near the counter.

"Carmine, buddy!" the tall, deep-voiced man said. He extended his arms as if he were going to hug him. Carmine lumbered up to men as if he had some weights attached to his ankles. He kicked some of the tootsies and glass out of the way. The littler guy, who was real red and veiny in his face at that point, pulled out a gun and rested it under his hand at the counter.

"What's it you two want?" Carmine spoke straight at them, violence in his voice.

"Haha! What we want?" The tall one laughed. "We don't want nothin'. We're just the messengers, Carmie."

"Aight, Moon." Carmine's tone backed down. "Who's your red-faced friend here?"

"Micky Monteri from Butler. We call him The Broom." Carmine waited, and the big one continued. "The Broom here cleans up messes real good. And Carmie . . . looks like you're a big, big mess." His finger wagging, he broke out into hysterical laughter.

I laid my head on the ground. The off-white tiles felt cool on my hot, swollen face. I could see the three pairs of well-worn, wingtip oxfords from under the shelves.

"Damn it, Moon! I gave you everything I got!"

"Boss knows you are lyin'. All yinz here in Mahoning are lyin'. What do you think happened to Covert, Carmine? Letin' that boy use your phone? You do realize what family he comes from right?"

"What was I supposed to do?! Turn him away? Yea, right, that'd-a been better."

"Yinz has got to pay up."

The Broom clicked his gun.

Wap, wap, wap. Someone banged on the door.

"Open up!" a muffled voice commanded from the outside. It was the fuzz. You can always tell the police-holler by their ridiculous "I'm-here-I'm-not-afraid-I'm-incharge-even-though-I-have-no-idea-what-I'm-doing" intonation. After Ang pointed that out to me, I couldn't unhear it.

Carmine answered, "Just a moment." He pushed Moon to the side and went for the door. When he unlocked it, it swung open.

"Sorry there, officer. It's about time I get that latch fixed. Or else my business is going to drop real fast," Carmine joked. By this point The Broom had grabbed a broom and was sweeping up the Tootsies.

There was a long pause. "Having some kind of problem here?" the officer asked. His voice carried a wave-like roll to it, and according to his vowels, he wasn't from around here. From my vantage point on the floor, I also noticed his abnormally large shoes. Shiny shoes. As he slapped in the door, it was obvious that those shoes were at least two-sizes too big, maybe even three. The officer's eyes shifted over to the Broom and his broom.

"No problem, just had a little accident," Moon kindly insisted.

The officer pulled back the corners of his mouth real hard. Suddenly, he stuck out his hand in the general direction of the men for a shake. "Well, I'm Officer Steve Subdolo. Pleasure to meet yinz."

The men paused, and finally Carmine reached out and shook.

All that tension lit some kind of fire in my bones. I had to move. I slowly moved onto my knees transcending the Wonderbreads. This was my chance. Those fools are gonna know, I assured myself, that everything they did and said I saw. I sure as hell will make them pay.

"Go ahead and take care of these fellas first, then I have some questions for you, after," Subdolo suggested to Carmine.

I imagined myself grabbing a whipped cream out of the refrigerator and slamming the door shut. Everything would go silent. The Broom's broom would stop. I'd walk out of the aisle toward them, whipped cream in one hand and Tootsie in the other. I cannot describe the immense pleasure I felt in that moment just imagining the fear I could instill in them all. The only time I felt that same breathless, electrifying burst of terror in my blood was when I jumped over that waterfall into the little hidden pond out by Hillsville.

Last summer was the first time I went to Hillsville—and hopefully the last time. Dad sent Nicky and Ang out there for something, and after three solid minutes of pleading, I finally gave up, snuck into the trunk of the station wagon, and revealed myself when we passed the quarries. At the first house in town, one old prune-looking guy stared at us as we drove past, and I mean start-to-finish stared at us. Out there, all the *dagos* shoot the breeze on their front porches like us, but they do it on rocking chairs with rifles next to them and statues of St. Mary housed in halved, old bathtubs in their front lawns. You would have thought we'd driven straight into Transylvania. On the way back Angelo convinced Nicky to stop the car so he could show me the little pond and the waterfall. The two of us traipsed for several minutes on an overgrown path with I'd say a hundred jagger bushes. Once we got to the falls, Ang dared me to jump off the top. I wanted to resist, but he said that he did all the time, and then he suggested that since I was just a girl, maybe I shouldn't, maybe when I'm older. And that drove me mad. That's when all that fire got in my bones, so I scrabbled up there faster than I could think about it. When my legs extended and my feet had just left the stone, I felt that glorious terror. Nicky was pissed when I got back all soaking wet. He made me ride in the trunk again.

In my imagination Carmine spoke. "Hey Rosie, you got everything you need?" He said while his startled face struggled not to contort.

"Yep, I got it." I wouldn't look at Subdolo. I'd just pass him. I'd walked up to the Broom, gliding on a sea of Tootsies. He'd stand there straight-faced staring into my eyes. I'd stare back. What would come over me right then, I don't know. I'd stop in front of him and stick out my hand. He would look down at the lone Tootsie I held. His hand would come off of the broom handle and pluck it out of my hand.

Then I'd say, "You do a pretty good job cleaning up messes." I'd slam my coins on the counter and head for the street.

That's when the fear hit. I heard some tremendous squawking coming from outside, some birds going at it. I stayed kneeling on the floor, immoveable. After a rather short conversation the ever gullible Officer Subdolo clunked out the door. Moon, Broom, and Carmine silently ascended to a more secluded place. I left without paying. Again.

When I rounded the corner, I peeked back into the alley where the squawks had come from. A little tuft of blue feathers rested in the middle of the gravel. Blue Jays. I peered into the tuft—no bird, just some feathers. My head rotated as I started to stand up. About two feet away, lay a severed leg, bird leg that is, claw and all, but no dead bird in sight. Thinking about a one-legged Blue Jay flying around Mahoningtown was kind of delightful, I'm not going to lie. I imagined it trying to sit on a fence, or a telephone wire, or a gutter. Then I decided to get home.

I called up Char in the morning and canceled our line drive. I did want to see her, and didn't want to let her down, but my vacant brain wouldn't let me. So I told her I had to go in and clean up the shop instead. And I did. Popi buffed the shoes, and I dusted and straightened and wiped and swept—all in silence. I knew that task would be silent and monotonous. Going through the shoes pair by pair required nothing from me, and its repetitive familiarity distracted me from the immense gloom that draped over my heart.

After I shuffled home, it became very apparent that Grandma had whipped up an elderberry pie without me knowing. It's not that I had a chance to smell its glorious scent wafting through the house or anything. I had swung open the door, dashed in—in fear of the machete-like edge—and had seen Nicky and Angelo flying across the hall from the dining room into the living room. Nicky had a piece of pie in his hand at the end of an over-extended elbow, precisely opposite Angelo. Ang pushed him around and lurched for the pie every now and again. As they tumbled about like squirrels over a nut, I chased them from room to room just for the sheer entertainment.

Angelo had a slight advantage on Nicky, since he was a few inches taller and had a serious wingspan, but it didn't seem to matter. Nicky didn't play games for the heck of it.

Tiny sheets of pastry flitted through the air. "Grandma's gonna kill you guys!" I yelled. She was one clean woman. Yet, I hoped that wouldn't stop them. It didn't.

Angelo had a nature of reckless impulsivity. Nicky had a heart of stone, dead-set and unwilling to cooperate. They flitted about congenially battling one another, handling chaos in their distinctive ways, just like when Angelo wrecked Nicky's best friend's car—the first time.

That time, Nicky had been hanging out in the living room, with these two girls from Youngstown. I stayed in the kitchen so I wouldn't have to talk to them or be un-included from their conversations or told to leave in some passive-aggressive way. When I chose to draw or read in the kitchen at times like this, I avoided a lot of trouble and still got to eavesdrop.

As it turned out, Nicky had driven to Youngstown. Now to me, Youngstown had been made out to be some kind of purgatory of thugs. All these villains hangin' out waiting, ya know, waiting to get back from wherever they came. Nicky tended to date girls from out there. I thought maybe he was just trying to save them, or perhaps to them he could be anybody he wanted—free of any trapping familial history. So anyhow Nicky picked up these two girls with the car of his best friend, Nicky Alex, a Syrian guy who lived across the street. Nicky A. worked until 7:30, so I guess our Nicky had to go pick up the girls by himself. Then after Nicky A. got off work, they were supposed to pick him up and go out or something.

Angelo sat in living room with the three of them. The girls didn't seem to be giving him the time of day. He tried to exude every ounce of coolness that he could muster up—I could tell from his voice. But the girls joked about his purple shirt. He, in all seriousness, made the claim that the shirt was periwinkle, not purple. Nicky probably agreed with him, but he didn't say anything. Instead, he changed the subject.

"I should probably head out—pick up Nicky," Nicky said. I imagined him looking at his watch. "Hang out here and we'll pick you up on the way back."

"I can get him!" Angelo chirped.

"No you can't," Nicky rebutted.

"I can drive. You've seen me."

"You only have a permit."

A five-second pause. The rough-voiced girl chimed in, "I can go with him." She sounded old enough to be driving around, so I figured it would probably be fine.

"Well, uh." Nicky paused again. "Yeah, guess that'd be fine." Some keys jingled. "Just don't wreck the car."

Angelo sighed. "I won't."

The front door opened and shut.

Not even eight minutes passed when the front doorknob clinked, and the whole door
slammed up against the wall. There was this crazy, raspy, hacking-up-a-lung type breathing— heaving in and out, in and out, super fast. I darted into the hallway to find out what the heck was going on. Nicky and I turned into the hall at the same time. The lung-hacker was Angelo, hands on his knees, heaving, trying to catch his breath.

"Ang! What're you doin'?" Nicky yelled.

Just heaving.

"Don't tell me," Nicky shut his eyes and spoke calmly, "Do not tell me you wrecked the car."

"I . . . I . . ." Angelo breathed out, "I wrecked the car."

"Damn it, Ang. Where's Millie?" Millie was the rough-voiced girl.

"I left her there." Heave. "In the car."

"You what?"

"Well, she hit her . . . her head." Heave. " . . . on the dash."

"And you left her there? Passed out?" Nick rested his forehead against the wall. "Anyone see you?"

Angelo nodded. "Had to swerve and miss a truck."

"Change shirts with me and come on!" So there they went stripping down and swapping clothes for some ungodly reason.
Nicky, Angelo, the other girl from Youngstown, and I took off out the door, kind of speed walking down the road. I could see that policemen had already arrived at the scene. Blue and red lights flashed off their faces.

While we walked, Nicky said to Angelo, "Tell me everything that happened."

"I was going down Elm and this dump truck pulled out from Baker without his lights on, so I didn't see'm till the last minute. I had to swerve to miss him, and I ran into the cord holdin' up the telephone pole."

"All right."

"There he is!" shouted the driver of the truck—at least, I presumed he was the driver, judging by his Navy-blue onesie.

"Which man?" a police officer asked.

The driver pointed. "That kid there, in the purple shirt."

I looked over at Nicky, who now wore the periwinkle shirt, and realized the motives behind the whole bit about changing clothes. Nicky passed the officers and the driver and went straight for the car. When he pulled on the door, it kind of rattled open. He ducked inside and put his face in front of Millie's while the rest of us watched through the window. She seemed awake now, talking back to him and all. One policeman was trying to help her out of the car, but the other policeman badgered Nicky. You know, trying to "get the facts."

"What's your name, boy?"

"Nicholas Luce."

The more stern of the officers spoke. "Ah, Luce boy, eh?" He looked askance at Nicky. "Tell me what happened here."

Nicky retold the story that Angelo had told him. The officers exchanged looks and then looked back at the driver in the jumpsuit.

The less stern officer told Nicky, "You failed to mention that you didn't have your lights on."

The stern officer kept narrow eyes on his prey. "Why'd you leave the scene of the accident?"

Nicky sounded calm. "We were just heading out to pick up a friend from work. So, I had to run home and give him a call to let him know that we were in an accident and we'd be late getting him."

The officers exchange glances again. Seemed like a good answer to me. I figured they were thinking that, too. Then they started working out the details of what needed to be done. This was fairly boring, and I suspected that it was not going to get any more interesting. So I began my pilgrimage back to the house. No use of standing outside in the dark listening to a boring conversation only to have a few mosquito bites to show for it.

A few days later I saw Nicky leaning up against the porch rail reading a letter. The envelope's tattered edges hung down. "Whatcha got there, Nicky?" I asked.

He didn't answer.

Dad had apparently heard me. He rolled out from under Nicky Alex's car and surveyed the scene. "Whatcha got, Nicky?" he asked.

Nicky bit his lower lip. "This letter says I owe the city of New Castle $400. For the wreck."

Dad swung his hands up under his head. "Hm-m."

"Says that this is for the price of a new telephone pole and a transformer. But, lemme tell ya," his voice raised and his hands swung out to the sides, "that's the same old pole down there. They haven't replaced anything."

"Four hundred? How you gonna pay for that? You don't have any money," Dad so graciously pointed out.

"I'm not payin' it at all! I'm going down to the court house to talk to them." And just like that, he was off.

An hour and a half later, when Nicky returned, Dad said, "Well?"

"Didn't pay it," Nicky replied.

"What?"

Nicky nodded. "I told them that the same old pole was there and that they should charge me only *after* they replace it. And I told them that when they do replace it I wanted the old pole. The lady there was like, 'What are you going to do with the pole?' And I said, 'Doesn't matter, I just want it.' And I left."

"What?" Dad stared at him. "Why would you want the old pole?"

"Da-a-a-ad. It's a matter of principle. They've got some kind of rogue telephone pole swindling going on, and I'm not playin' their game."

"They are just going to keep pestering you."

"Don't care. Eventually they got to stop. I mean, if they replace the pole, I'll pay, but if they don't, I'm not giving them anything."

After that ploy actually worked, Nicky was pretty certain about the way society ought to be handled. The thing is, a month later, when Angelo had his full license, he wrecked the station wagon again: same telephone pole, same truck, same transformer, same letter. Angelo lasted about twenty-two hours before he got a loan from Carmine and marched down to the court house to pay it. Then he spent the next six months workin' for Carmine to pay it off.

Concerning the pie, I knew Angelo would give up, or rather just give in. And as things turned out, by the time Grandma walked in from drinking her afternoon coffee with Mrs. Siciliano, I was happily seated at the kitchen table eating that very piece of elderberry pie.

CHAPTER **12**

I awoke to yet another gray morning. Sitting on the edge of my bed, I stared at the clouds, those familiar heavy sinking, oppressive dollops. Grandma's voice booming up the stairs interrupted my thoughts. I tell you, the woman was small, but her tiny frame had no bearing on outrageous register of her voice. I mean the stairs creaked, the blinds shook, the trusses shifted, and my gray soul was struck by what seemingly felt like goodhearted lightning.

"You wanna panacake-a?" she yelled.

I wasn't sure if she was talking to me or somebody else. All I knew was, yes! Of course I wanted a pancake. I stood and swung open the door. At that moment, Angelo swung open his and Nicky's door, and we stood, staring each other down under our door frames. A motion out the window caught my eye, and I swear I saw a tumbleweed roll past and swirl of dust kick up. I pulled my a red handkerchief over my nose.

Angelo adjusted his ten-gallon hat and clicked a spur on the ground. A hawk, circling our daring duel, let out a call. Angelo and I stared each other in the eyes. Then he rushed to the stairs, but I leapt onto his back before he could get away. Thinking back on it, that could have easily been the end of Grandma—if he had fallen down the stairs with me on his back, a real-live tumble weed. Luckily he braced himself on the railing while I hung from his neck. My legs slipped off his waist and hung down as he slowly dragged me down the stairs.

Grandma reprimanded us in Italian while Nicky stood at the sink making some coffee. I tried hard not to laugh. Saturday mornings were the best. Grandma's head tipped back and forth and her hands whipped all over the place. I peered over her shoulder, down the hall and out the living room window. Smoke fogged up the window panes, but I could see vague outlines of men. Dad and Popi were both sitting out on the porch—Popi on the swing and Dad on his chair.

Soon enough Grandma finished. Angelo followed her into the kitchen, but I hightailed it down the hall and onto the porch, which smelled like a pool hall. I basically had to swim over to Popi. Dad smiled with his eyes when I lumbered past his teary-eyed smoke haze.

The big pouches beneath Dad's eyes sagged. His eyelids were beginning to give way to gravity. Not to mention that the amount of skin clinging beneath his eyebrows was way more than slack needed for him to blink, so it kind of hung over, supported by his eyelashes. I took full responsibility for that. As a kid I spent many mornings trying to wake up Dad by flapping open his eyelids and holding them up with my fingers. His dead eyes would just stare out as if nothing changed, so I would shut them and then do it again—until his eyes would suddenly and quite terrifyingly shift to the side.

Before I had the chance to get situated on the swing, Grandma knocked on the window to let us know breakfast was ready. Dad stood and put out his cigarette. Popi did the same, and I followed them into the kitchen.

We sat in there talking and eating and telling stories. Oddly enough, Angelo never looked up. Even when Dad talked, Ang didn't ever make an acknowledgment—no laugh or smile, or roll of the eyes, or joke. Nothing. When we finished up the last of the fried eggs and pancakes, to my dismay, Mugga came strolling in. I just didn't like being around that guy. There was always something no good about him, and even though Hog was a complete sociopath, I did kind of believe him about the oddity of Mugga's business endeavors. But of course, Grandma was delighted to see him, not because she liked him all that much, I'd assume, but because delight was the appropriate reaction to a guest coming over, even an uninvited one. She pulled out another chair and slipped a pancake off of Popi's plate onto a fresh one for Mugga. Popi didn't even object. He just looked at Grandma over his glasses and picked up his coffee cup.

"Oh, wow. Thank you, Rosemary!" Mugga gushed. Sometimes I forgot Grandma and I shared a name.

Angelo got up, exited the kitchen, and went out the back door. He didn't even speak to Mugga or even thank Grandma. Angelo was generally the nice one of all of us.

After we all finished up, Popi and I collected the plates and coffee cups and random utensils and set them over by the sink. I looked out back through the kitchen window. And Angelo was not to be seen. It's not like the kitchen window actually gave a good visual of the alleyway anyhow. So I set down my mostly finished glass of milk and started toward the back door. Out of the corner of my eye I saw Dad pick up the milk and finish it.

I spotted Angelo out in the alleyway, leaning up against the siding, smoking a jack. I, still hidden by the door frame, peeked my head around the corner.

"Didn't know you smoked, Ang," I said.

He just looked down—didn't say anything.

I stepped down the two cement stairs off the back door onto the dry, rocky back-of-the-house-nothing-to-be-ashamed-of ground. A few plants poked up between rocks about a third of them had little white flowers.

"What's that smell?" I looked at him quizzically. "Like a squirrel just bathed in Pine-Sol."

He laughed.

I leaned against the house beside him, both of us facing the alleyway. "What's going on? You look bad." My lip quivered.

Angelo just shrugged his shoulders, and puffed out some smoke. I mean I couldn't blame him for keeping to himself. For what it's worth, I kept quiet too.

"Hate livin' here." Angelo puffed out with the next exhale. I said nothing, and he continued. "There's just nothing more for me here. Nothing. And there's no way out."

"What about wrestling? And that recruiter from Kent State and stuff?"

"Phff. Who cares."

"What do you mean? They'll pay for you to go to school and everything. And then you'll be free. You can move anywhere, get a job doin' whatever."

"They won't take me."

"Sure they will! You're like the best boxer in the Tri-county, and who knows maybe even the state!"

"Not any more."

"What?"

"Not any more."

"You lose or something. Gee, its just one match . . . "

He cut me off, "Coach dropped me."

"What?"

He looked over at me. "Yeah, that's what I said!"

"Why would he do that?!" I screeched, "He's been coaching you forever, and you guys are like, like friends." Ang said nothing. I pushed forward. "Did he say?"

Angelo dropped his cigarette and pounded it into the dirt. He leaned down to my height and peered daggers at my face. "It's . . ." He looked up over my head toward the back door and window and back down. His face softened. "It's just something with Dad. Coach said he couldn't be seen lookin' like he was in with him."

"With him? WHAT'D HE DO?" I yelled.

He slammed his hand over my mouth, "Shut up! Geez!" He seemed to catch himself because he softened too. "Just don' worry about it, Rose, all right?" He patted me on the shoulder and walked down the alleyway and out of sight.

The Pine-Soled-squirrel smell vanished in the wind, and I was left to breathe oxygen again. I stayed there leaning up against the back of the house. As I rubbed my feet together, the rocks slid around under my shoes.

Angelo never got any honor around there, or at least that is what he seemed to set his mind on—and he'd find it.

Nicky, on the other hand, did win a lot of attention from Dad and all, but that was just how it was. I didn't care so much at that point. Nicky was the oldest. He was the one with Dad's name. But I just didn't know what the big deal was for Ang. He was real popular with those successful humans, ya know, all the football players and cheerleaders at school, and not to mention his boxing launched him into Mahoningtown stardom. People liked him for sure. Some of the girls even worshipped him. I'd say that if Mahoningtown was a person, he liked Ang.

Most people were just kind of leery of Nicky, though I reckoned Nicky didn't deserve it. He just had a look about him, like he was up to no good. It was a face that made you want to scream, "Wipe that look of your face!" People might have liked him more if they couldn't see his face—like when you go to confession and there is a little screen between you and the priest. You can't see each other. There's something strange about it. The screen and the faceless voice make it easier to talk.

Another breeze swept through the alley. I turned to the stairs and entered through the back door. The TV resounded from the living room. Everybody stood watching as a monotone-news-voice articulated something with vigor. Their tense bodies blocked the screen. I walked around the mass and sat in the rocking chair, wondering what they were watching.

A reporter was talking. "After the body was found, investigators confirmed that this, indeed, was the body of Richard Charles Covert, murdered . . ." An image of the burnt once-house-now-ruins flashed across the screen. "Covert's home was destroyed by what was previously discerned as an accidental electrical fire, but now Lawrence County Police have reopened the case for further investigation."

A voice recording of Officer Deleone sprayed through the speakers. "Yes, this is a tragic case, and we are doing our best here at Lawrence County Sheriff's office to get this sorted out." The reporter flashed back on the screen. "Was Richard Covert's murder intentionally disguised by the fire at his home? Officials have begun to make their investigation. All individuals connected to this case will be questioned. We will keep you updated on this story's trajectory." Popi beamed off the TV.

A knock at the front door made me jump. No one spoke. Nicky headed to the bathroom, while I followed Popi to the door.

An officer of the law flashed his badge. "Hello, sir," he said. "I'm Officer Steve Subdolo with the Lawrence County Police. I need to speak with Nicholas Luce. Is he here at the moment?"

Popi kind of swayed before turning around to face me. He reeled across the hall in a trance, like he didn't even see me there. Clearly he wasn't going to find Nicky, so it was up to me.

I nodded to the big-shoed officer. "Yeah. I'll go get him for you." I didn't even invite the man in. Instead, I turned and shuffled down the hall. That's when I saw Grandma taking it all in. She stood in the kitchen, one arm around her ribs and the other stroking her bottom lip. My head started to feel funny. I felt like I was walking in slow-motion. I watched my feet extend in front of me and support my weight. But they were someone else's feet. I knocked on the bathroom door.

"Yeah?" Nicky's voice answered me.

I couldn't figure out what to say; it was like the English language evaded me. "An officer's at the door for you." I tried to say as nonchalantly as possible.

Nicky opened the door. He was drying his hands on his pants as he came out. His face looked white as a sheet, yet he sauntered down the hall to the door where Popi now stood.

"Hello, son, Officer Steve Subdolo here." He flashed the badge again. "I'm here with a warrant for your arrest."

Popi's hand slammed up against the wall. He stumbled backward. Tears welled up in his eyes.

"It's all right, Popi." Nicky leaned over to put his face in front of Popi's. "We'll get this sorted out."

I tried to vanish down the hall, but my knees locked up mid-stride.

"What's this all about, sir?" I heard Nicky ask the policeman. He sounded like Dad the way he said it, like a man. I turned back to hear Steve's answer.

Subdolo straightened up. He rested his right hand on his waist, near his holster. "I think you know what I'm here for, son."

I found the word "son" extremely annoying.

"I'm sorry sir, but I'm not exactly sure what you mean."

"We need to take you in for some questioning for the Covert case," Subdolo sheepishly answered. His voice wobbled as he continued, "You're the closest witness to the events, son." A damned, dumb, cognitively forced smile stretched across his lips, and his eyes darted around from face to face.

Again, a surge of fire shot through my bones. "Excuse me officer! But it seems like you are going to have to take me, too!" I stepped around Popi up to Nicky's side and extended my wrists to be cuffed.

This time Subdolo gave an abhorrent, crooked, kind of cutesy-cutesy smile at me. He kind of hunched down to my eye level and answered, "Oh, no, darling, I only need Nicholas." He stood back up and started cuffing Nicky, who just passively allowed him.

"Well," I continued as I pushed between Nicky and Subdolo, "if it is true that you are collecting witnesses, I've got some stuff to say."

Just then Subdolo's partner emerged from the cop car and made his way down the side walk to our door.

"Having some trouble here?" the tall dark Italian boomed. His voice was deep and wide and like something one hears only in a dream.

"Yes, officer. We are," I insisted. I could see Nicky looking down at me with a worrisome glare. "You are collecting witnesses to the Covert case . . ." the officer got closer to me, and a serum of fear pumped through my veins. "I was, um, I was in Covert's field, down by the river that whole morning." A vision of the burning soot fluttered down in front of my eyes. My hands shook.

"Mm-m. Is that so?" Officer Deleone sounded skeptical as he picked through his notebook. "Doesn't seem like we have any records of girls your age on the case."

I stared up to his eyes. He didn't remember me? Deleone didn't look at me, actually he hadn't flashed me even the slightest glance during the entire interaction. He reached over me to Dad and extended his hand for a shake. "Thank you for your time." Dad didn't move a muscle. Deleone dropped his hand and grabbed the chain between Nicky's cuffed wrists, pulling him down the porch stairs like he was some kind of criminal.

I resisted. "Exc—" But a hand came from behind me and cupped itself around my mouth. It was Dad's. I could tell by the smell. My arms dropped limp.

I watched as the officers took Nicky to their car. My brother didn't look back. They opened the back door to the vehicle and shoved him in. And something boiled in my lungs. I shook Dad off of my face and started down the stairs. I didn't know where I was going, but I sure as hell wasn't staying there. If Ang had been standing there with us I knew, I really did know, that I surely would have killed him.

"*Rosie!*" Dad hollered.

I turned around to face the three of them—Grandma, Popi and Dad. We all just stood there, staring at each other.

CHAPTER **13**

C icadas work as traveling musicians. Every seven years they came to Mahoningtown. 1968 was one of those years. As I stood on the path, trees hummed the tunes of a secret orchestra. Birds danced on the branches and talked among themselves. Several squirrels seemed to be in an argument. They tumbled over each other and flew through the air from tree to tree.

Char trekked three steps ahead of me. In "P.A.," forests flood the landscape. I mean we were technically in the city, being on Union Hill and all, but the woods spread like ivy along the roads, between the fences, and through the yards.

Char and I have taken that particular woodly path many times. We took it after the US government elected her brother for the draft. We took it when I got my third consecutive "F" on a spelling test for Mrs. Murckle in second grade, but honestly, that was overtly the school's fault. How was I supposed to know how to sound out words "phonetically" when my first-grade teacher, Mrs. Turkle, oddly enough, had such a wacky Louisiana drawl that I myself ended up with a slight southern accent by the end of October?

We took that path on Charlotte's birthday the previous year, and we took it when she landed a gig in the circus act. Some guy came to her dance class and picked her out. His troupe did tricks like spinning plates while doing summersaults. My favorite was the one where Char jumped off a ladder onto a trampoline and flipped forward, landing in a handstand atop that guy's sky-stretched arms.

My feet crunched the twigs and the leaves rejected by the ancient branches. We stored up a lot of memories under those layers of dirt. Those grandfather trees must have sucked up all the usual, day-to-day memories that we so quickly forgot.

Char turned back to me. "You suppose one day I could be a trapeze artist?"

"Ha!" I felt myself crack a smile. "What made you think of that?"

"Squirrels." Her finger pointed to a rustling clump of limbs above us.

"Ha-ha!"

She wiggled her eyebrows. "But seriously, wouldn't that be great?"

I know she didn't really mean it. She just liked to dream sometimes, like she was a character in one of those books she read. Both she and I knew she would never leave New Castle. She was too afraid.

"I think maybe for you . . . You're kind of doin' it now."

"You mean the acrobat act with Mr. Clark?" She turned forward and continued agilely maneuvering around low-hanging branches and jagger bushes.

"You *are* pretty good, ya know. Maybe you could audition for the real time circus next time they *swing* by."

Char turned her gaze back to me and seemed to study my face or one of those eternal split seconds, probably unsure if I was serious or sarcastic. I pursed my lips in an unsuccessful effort to hide my laughter.

"You, my friend, get a real kick outta yourself, don't you!" said Char.

We passed behind the last great obstacle, a giant ever-growing rose bush at the edge of the Luneskis' yard. Hilda Luneski was Charlotte's great aunt, and beyond that ghastly rose bush lay her backyard. Hilda had this arbor next to her garden, which sheltered a little table and two chairs beneath its viney trusses. If it were the right time of year, brimming bunches of grapes would sway down to arms' reach.

We sat down. Char tilted back on her chair and plucked through some of the vines dangling overhead. I looked at her and wondered. Did she really pass out and miss the whole thing? Why didn't I pass out too? Why did I have to see it all? I had no answers.

"These vines sure do have a lot of leaves," Char stated, still tilted back and looking up. "You'd think the leaves would be more blatantly useful."

"The Syrians find them useful," I reminded her. "You've been down to Greek fest—'member Nicky Alex's mum?"

She nodded. "But most people just like the fruit, you know, and most of the plant, most of the year, is mostly leaves." She plucked off a clump of grape leaves and whipped them into the air. "So many leaves!" She laughed.

"Hello Charlotte! Hello!" A raspy voice erupted from the house. And Mrs. Hilda Luneski, whom Charlotte calls "Great-auntie" and whom I secretly refer to as "the woman in white," bounced down the steps from her screen-covered back porch. The woman in white kind of moved like a grape herself, bouncing about with juice-filled buoyancy. But, when Mrs. Luneski wasn't bouncing around the house or bounding through her garden or frolicking to the mailbox with that crazy spring, she had a rather ghostly appearance. Come to think of it, I don't suppose I ever saw her wearing an actual color. All her cotton house dresses ranged from ebony to cream to egg-shell to vanilla and, well, to plain-old white. Her stance in those ghostly situations was cold, still, and perfectly straight—her mouth expressionless, eyes wide, arms and hands slightly extended out from the sides, open as if waiting to take flight. Even through the months of summer gardening, her pale skin remained pale. She often wore long-sleeves and hats when outdoors. That translucent skin next to the white cotton and the strikingly round eyes had an I'm-seeing-a-ghost or I-am-a-ghost expression written all over it. And that is how she had come to be known, by me, only to me, and on the rare occasion to Char, as "the woman in white."

She came bounding off the back porch. "Hello, Charlotte!"

"And, Rosie," Char replied, reminding her of my name, which never really found a good sticking place.

Hilda made her way across the drive and through the grass. I rested against the table and moved my hand up to my jaw, doing my best to cover the stitched wound at the right corner of my mouth. The last thing I wanted was to explain my injury to an old woman who didn't know my name, who looked simultaneously like grape and ghost, and who I knew had a tendency to blow small things out of proportion and make me feel extremely awkward at receiving her rudeness that she disguised as kind attention.

"Rosie, dear, how is grandma doing?" the woman in white puffed out while holding up her dress to romp through the grass. "I haven't seen her since bingo in June."

"Oh, she's doin' good."

"Working on some berry canning, I assume?"

I nodded. "Yeah, here and there."

"Great Jiminie, it has been quite the summer for strawberries! I can't seem to keep up with the amount Uncle Earnest brings home." Her face fixed forward, expectant, as if I had something more to contribute to the conversation. However, I didn't.

Charlotte chimed in, on cue. "Rosie and I," repeating my name again, "were just talking about how we can't wait for all of these grapes to come in." Though, we did had not actually discussed that as far as I could remember.

"What are you girls up to today?" Her aunt responded as if Charlotte had not even spoken.

"Just having a walk before Rosie goes in to the shoe shop."

Hilda's eyes looked wide with excitement. "Has Grandpa got you working in the store now too?" Her voice warbled like a Yellow-rumped Warbler in the heart of July, and she didn't wait for an answer. "I remember when your Daddy started working there. He was about your age." Her wide eyes narrowed and followed the wind off into some distant memory. "Oh, how time flies."

"Yeah, Popi's got me doing inventory and cleaning and what not. Nothin' real exciting yet."

"Well you've got to start somewhere."

"Yep, I mean, really I don't mind, it's nice."

Hilda shifted her focus to her niece. "And how about you, Charlotte, any plans today?"

Char shrugged. "Not too much, maybe helping out Mom in the garden a little, and reading."

"Oh, look at you," the woman in white doted. Her gross sentimentality was the apex of her charm. "The girl who's always reading. What books are you reading these days?"

"*The Adventures of Huckleberry Finn.*"

"O-o-oh, how interesting." The woman in white probably never read about those adventures. I heard girls didn't read back when she was a spring chicken.

Char offered, "Yes, its pretty good so far. I just started yesterday."

"And that means you are already halfway right?" I joked, but seriously.

Char's eyes rolled from the woman in white to me, dead pan. Char read fast, I mean like Wilma Rudolph fast.

"Well, I won't bother you two any longer." The woman in white adjusted herself to travel back across the yard.

"Not a bother at all!" Char said, pleasantly.

"Enjoy your day. It's beautiful," Mrs. Luneski chimed as she began her buoyant journey back.

"Thanks great-auntie. You too!" Char looked back up at the leaves. But I watched that hoot of an aunt comically parade herself through the yard.

She stopped and looked across the field into the woods. She transformed into the ominous and serene woman in white for just that moment and then bounced right back into her grapey self. Unbelievable.

"Rosie." Char looked down, then back at me. She sounded alarmed "What's going on?"

I looked at her quizzically. My insides moved from a solid state to liquid goo.

"I'm mean you haven't seemed quite yourself for while, and now with Nicky . . . I just . . ." Char knew me too well.

I looked at her stiffly. "Um, I don't know." There was no way in hell I could explain the fog that had been suffocating my brain and how my incessant gasping made me feel like I was almost always on the edge of screaming.

She gazed at me with an expression of knowing my disclaimer wasn't the truth.

I looked down at the cobble stone beneath our feet and kicked a few rocks out of the crevices.

"Rosie. If you ever want to talk about anything, you know . . . " she offered.

I nodded. "Yeah, yeah. I know." I kept my eyes fixed on the ground. I suddenly felt like I was going to explode. I felt like I was a grape, and her was foot squishing me, albeit tenderly, onto the cobble stone. As much as I wanted to explode all over and tell her about the Italians, the slit-up guy in the field, who I saw out there, and how I was so, so angry, and Carmine hiding on the pew, and the Tootsie rolls, I just couldn't. I just couldn't put her through that. She cared about me too much. The last thing I wanted to do was impart to her the same head-spinningness that I endured. And that's exactly what would have happened had I spoken.

I stared out to Mrs. Luneski's house. The sunlight shined off of the back windows and heat radiated off of the aluminum overhang covering the stairs of her tiny back porch. That light and heat kind of spoke to me. It made me feel okay—for a moment. "Your mum starting school in the fall?" I looked back up to her.

"Yep," Char answered. She had taken the bait, so she chuckled. "Yeah, she tried to tell my Dad the other night, but luckily he was too sloppy drunk to really get mad. I don't think it could sink into his head, you know?"

"I guess that worked out!" I laughed.

She looked down. "Yep, it worked out."

I looked down at my watch. "We should probably start back. Last thing I want is Popi cussing me out in the mother-tongue." I double-raised my eyebrows and cracked a smile. I rose, and Char followed me into the woods.

"Rose, you know, if you ever need to just get out, you know you could always come stay with us for a while."

I swiveled around. "What? . . . Why would I ever want to come stay with you? To be made a point of by your drunk-ass dad?" As soon as those words came out of my mouth, I knew I was no good, couldn't keep a friend if I tried. I swiveled forward and tromped over a jagger bush. Char remained silent all the way through the woods. Once in her yard, I traipsed over to the telephone pole where I had left my bike.

"See you tomorrow?" Char asked.

I turned to look at her, the first time since my remark.

"The line?" she continued.

I didn't deserve her. "Yeah, yeah, sounds good."

"I'll meet you at your place. How's that sound?" she asked.

I nodded somberly. "See you then."

Before I finished rolling down Sunny Avenue, the surge of regret overwhelmed me, but there wasn't enough time to get down to St. Mary's and back over to the shop by 2:30. So I coasted down Sunny through Elm, and I almost made it around the corner onto Cascade before I had to manually operate the bike again. It wasn't a record, but it was still pretty good.

I rushed through my duties at the shop. I couldn't take the waiting period. I just needed to get it over and done with, get the past behind me. So when Popi was taking out the trash, I made my escape. He knew that I was leaving soon, so it wasn't like I was deserting him. I just needed to get out while he wasn't around, in order to avoid his interrogation concerning my whereabouts.

I leapt on my bike mid-stride. I suppose all that pent-up adrenaline pumped my legs. I arrived at St. Mary's with lightning speed. After skidding into the bushes, I threw my bike behind them. That's when I noticed something across the street. Two men emerged from a black Thunderbird, and both of them were looking at me. Suddenly, I had the dooming realization that they were following me. I had spun down there so quickly that I hadn't paid attention to the cars that passed. The man on the driver's side leaned against the car as he stood peering over at me. I slowly ascended the stairs to the church, keeping my eyes fixed on them. The second guy leaned back into the car, across the seat, and laid on the horn, giving it two good whirls. I slipped under the stone arch into the foyer—my heart pounding. Holy water. Crossed myself.

In the sanctuary I could see a small group huddled together up by the Mary statue. Father Piccolo sat among them. I felt choked by disgust, hatred even. Just to think people with their holy little lives could sit in there peacefully praying while I had to live in hell, but then again I guessed that their kind of lives were ones you got to live when God notices you. Father Piccolo stood up when he saw me.

"Rosie! How good to see you this evening!" shouted across the sanctuary.

I crossed along the pew, cussed to myself, and marched down the side aisle. Why couldn't he just let me slide into place inconspicuously?

"Have you come for the prayer group?" he asked.

I stopped next to the elaborately carved confessional. "I came to confess," I rather brazenly shouted back.

Piccolo patted one of the women on the shoulder and spoke softly to the group. I dove into my side of the booth and awaited Piccolo's arrival, which took nearly hours, it seemed.

Piccolo had just started to utter a syllable, but my hand was already in full swing to slap the wooden desk in front of me. A sharp crack echoed loud enough for parishioners to hear even outside the confessional. I saw through the screen dimly that the sound made Piccolo shift in his seat. It wasn't my intention to cut him off, but I did, and I was certainly glad about it. I just wanted to cut through the crap and get this damn weight off my chest. I slid the crucifix with its safety-pinned chain under the screen. "I stole this."

A long silence followed, but finally he asked, "You stole this?"

"Yes, and now I am returning it. I confess," I asserted. "I didn't know what I was doing at the time, and I still don't fully believe I actually stole it, for sure, but, I don't care. I just can't take it anymore."

With an endearing tone Piccolo responded. "What is it that you can't take, Rosie?"

"What do you mean?"

"You said that you 'can't take it.' What's 'it'?"

"My, um, my . . . family." Even I was shocked that that is what slipped from my tongue. I corrected the statement. "I stole this crucifix from a nun, and now my family has the malocchio. We're good people, I swear. We are, but I screwed it all up."

"Why do you think that?"

"It's judgment Father, you know! You're the one who preaches it all the time. I'm a complete, a complete fraud. I'm a deserter."

"Fraud? Rosie, you are not a fraud."

"Yes. Yes, I am. I'm a fraud and I'm a phony and I'm a sinner. And, here's the damned chain. Now uncurse us."

"Rosie, can I ask you a question?" Piccolo calmly asked.

My blood pressure, by that point, was through the roof, and my hands were shaking and my vision blurring and I was already ashamed that I said that stuff. But his soft, tender, put-you-to-sleep voice rushed at me like a warm breeze.

He continued, "What happened to make you think your family has the malocchio?"

I felt my face unhinge and my cheeks hang down. My shoulders untensed, and a slight tingle ran down my legs. "They're bad," my voice softly wavered, "I made them bad. Now, there is someone after us. I know it. I know it for sure," I whispered. "I hear them walking around our house at night. I seen them follow me here. I cursed us, I sinned, and now I can't get away from it."

"Excuse me for a moment." Piccolo left the confessional. I peeked out my door. He walked toward Mary and whispered something to a woman in the group. She immediately stood and ran to the back room, where the altar servers get ready. My feet tapped on the floor boards.

"Father, what is my penance?"

"Your penance is the Lord's prayer."

"How many?"

"Once."

"Once?" The crucifix lay shimmering before me. I lurched out of the confessional and ran out the front doors.

"Rosie!" Piccolo yelled.

I slid out the door, hopped through the flowerbed and hid myself under one of those burning bushes. Sirens rang in the distance. Soon enough, two police cars pulled up in front of the church. Deleone and Subdolo got out of one car and two other guys got out of the other. The four of them rushed into the church. I thought about sneaking back in and crawling under the pews. I imagined laying there listening to what they were saying. But I was too scared. I wasn't scared that I would get caught. I was just still scared that I had said the wrong thing. I told him too much. I wondered if

Piccolo told them about the guys that follow us, or if it was just about me. Am I gonna get locked up now? I wondered. I grabbed my bike and ran it down to the halfway house. After sliding it under the porch, I slipped under there too. And I watched events transpiring down the street.

It was only a few minutes before the police cars drove off, and Piccolo and the prayer group exited the church. Some left by foot. Some hopped in their respective vehicles. They vacated the premises. Piccolo lumbered away, alone. He seemed to be meandering, gazing upward at the darkening sky.

CHAPTER **14**

With the sun, I rose from my roughshod, wiry mattress. Mornings comforted more than sleep itself. Some rumblings reverberated downstairs, kindling a curiosity that drove me up, out, and down. A soft blue light filled the house. In the kitchen Dad gulped down some coffee. He wore his woods-gear and sleek mahogany rifle slung across his back.

"Dad" I caught his attention with my faint whisper. "Where you going?"

He swallowed down another gulp of coffee. Somehow. I mean, it was steaming right out of the cup, but Dad had a mouth of steel.

"Thought I'd check Nicky's traps for him."

"Can I come?"

"No."

"Why not?"

"I don't want you out there in those woods for a while."

"Dad . . . But I'll be with *you*."

He bid a downcast glance—the kind that sternly "recommended" the obvious. He set the mug back on the counter. I could see a few thimble-fulls of murky coffee slosh around the bottom. Those were for me. I figured I'd wait till he left to drink them though. He adjusted the rifle behind his back and walked toward the front door. The screen door slammed.

My coffee trickled down like bitter water, a taste which I had at first only endured now evoked a ritualized sense of joy. Mug in hand, I wobbled down the hall to the front door and stepped out onto the porch. Dad was already out of sight. I slumped down in his chair.

About twenty minutes passed before Jimmy Mancini came marching up the street. He told me he came speak with Popi. I let him inside to the now fully awakened house then scurried up the stairs. I could hear him and Popi talking in kitchen table while Grandma made what smelled like toast and coffee. I knew that I would hear them pretty clearly if I laid on the floor at the top of the stairs. But I also know that I would hear them exceptionally well if I went across the opening at the top of the stairs and hung my head between the rungs.

Jimmy had a nasally way of speaking that emphasized all the m's and n's. His New York accent was as thick as Grandma's Rice pudding, which was pretty thick. Utensils scraped on ceramic plates, cups knocked against tables, and chairs squeaked.

"Rooster" Jimmy said, "ya gonna have ta do somethin' about that boy of yours." He gulped down some liquid. "I mean, I heard they came fa Zullo's son a few years back . . . and thei' sayin' lil' Andre Carmidio didn't die in the Vietnaam wa' after oll."

Silence.

I didn't even know Carmine had a son, but I imagined that he was tall with dark brown wavy hair and wore soccer jerseys all the time—seemed like the kind of kid Carmine would father.

Jimmy continued, "Ya not gonna get outa this one, Roos."

"We-a make way. We-a find a way," Popi insisted.

"Roos. Ya unda' stand what I'm tellin' ya!" Jimmy's voice raised and nasal-ness heightened to a kind of piercing pinnacle. "They gonna come fo' yours too, Roos. Dant matter who ya are or what ya did for them in the ol'days."

"You believe everybawdy tell-a you. People just-a scared cuz all the fuss over Covert," Popi stated.

"And, Lightsey, Bongivni, and Vito before him, Roos. This isn't out'a nowhere! They on to us. We gotta pay fo'sins in our family's. Ain't no mercy."

Popi's voice transfigured into a type of cruel tone that I've never heard from him. This sharp edge put to shame all of the yelling I've heard from him over my past eleven years. "People a-talk, they're scared-a, no buddy gonna pull up a debt from years ago. I'm ashame-ed a'you Jimmy. Ashame-ed."

I tried to get my head out from between the rungs. I wanted to get out. Get out of there, but I was stuck. I didn't know what they were talking about, but I didn't care. I yanked my head between the bars, but my neck was up too far, where one of the spindles bent in and made the space more narrow than the diameter of my skull. My arms shook as they supported my body. I crouched low to the ground and let my head lower till it hit the magic spot. Only there could my head slip through without harm.

"Roos," Jimmy continued after a brief period of silence. "He did wrong ta dem. He left dem against his word. They don't fo-get, no matta if its dis time or da next. An the good Lord ain't gonna protect you like you did fo-im. An I did fo Mickey." He began to cry. "We done wrong, Roosie . . . You . . ."

I leaned my forehead on a rung. Then I slid down and rested my chin on the floor.

"We done wrong."

It's funny how things just come back to bite you, like those damned rungs. That hazel-eyed curiosity which drove like a fire propelling me toward those men in the black suits had finally blazed so big that it suffocated me. Some time in those past days, my own fascination seemed to be more of a bondage than delight. Instead of wanting to know more, I wanted to know less. I wanted to be wiped clean of any memory of those gangs of whispering suited fellows. And when I realized they'd been sitting in my kitchen all of those years, I just wanted to get out.

That evening they told us about Dad. Officer Steve Subdolo stopped by to let us know. Grandma answered the door. Angelo and I were sitting at the kitchen table. I had on my yellow blouse with the white trim. I was sorting Ang's old baseball cards, and Angelo was removing some kind of sticky substance from one of Dad's tools. The smell of rubbing alcohol still haunts me.

I laid awake that night for hours. I imagine everybody did. It was our first night without Dad in the house, but not like when he'd work a night shift. He wasn't coming back. It was dark. They said he had a heart attack out there in the middle of the woods. Around five, a fellow woodsman found him laying out by the deserted house where the lilies grew.

I wondered what he thought about out there, lying in the middle of that great green cathedral, dying alone.

Finally, dawn cracked its furious glow. I wasn't tired at all. I never got tired that night. I staggered down the stairs, accidentally hitting one squeak on the third from the bottom. Alarmed by the squeak, I tip-toed to the front door. The kitchen was quiet. The living room was quiet. If I hadn't known better, I would have guessed that the house was empty, abandoned like one of those rundown shacks on Baker Street.

The porch was real quiet, except for a couple cars and men on bikes riding down to the mill for the daylight shift. None of them turned their zombie eyes toward me, but what could I expect? Even some of their dusty windshields were still glazed with lingering dreams.

I walked over to Dad's chair and had a seat. The wind swept in with a spicy chill. For summer it was the beginning of the end. I thought that the fall-like briskness felt nice. It felt good on my eyeballs, which were abnormally hot.

Like on the mornings after I eat too many grapes, I couldn't fully open my eyes. My eyelids had puffed out. I shut them and sat still, save gliding my hands over the chair's bumps and ridges. Things feel a lot different with your eyes shut. A truck rumbled past. I plucked a fresh jack out of the silver box under Dad's chair. Dad's Bible sat on the stool next to the ash tray. I could see the end of the lighter, tucked under the front cover. I took it out and flicked the spark at the butt of that homemade cigarette. It warmed my mouth against the chilly air. I did my best to suck it in as hard as I could, but, of course, without letting the smoke touch the back off my throat. I immediately hacked out thick wind. The silk wafted up around my head. I did it again and again and again. I sucked and puffed until the divine smog was so thick around me that it draped a veil over my face.

Dad's spare cigarette rolled down the uneven stool top slope. I'd never given that jack a thought. I guess I was just accustomed to leaving that one there. Dad never moved it or gave it to anyone. I swear it had lain there for years, the same one. It just sat there waiting for some reason or another. It kindled in me a strange sense of friendliness, communion—a nearness of our two abandoned souls. I placed it back in its spot behind the Bible.

The chair legs tipped-back, guiding my head to rest against the exterior paneling in the familiar company of a toxic breeze.

The screen door slammed shut, which scared the bee-geebers out of me. I landed all four legs—bang—on the floor.

"Rosie, what the heck are you doin' out here this early? Have you been smoking?" Ang demanded.

"Please, please," I pleaded, "Do *not* tell Grandma!"

Hands on hips, he peered down at me. Two crinkled lines sunk between his eyebrows, and a little piece of his swept-back hair drooped forward and bounced off his forehead, landing atop his furry right brow.

"Where going?" I eagerly changed the subject.

"Out."

" . . . um." I looked around at the shadowy street.

"To work," he stated.

"Work? At the shop?"

"No. We need *actual* money, Rosie." He spoke with an agitated grown-up tone. "Popi can't get us out."

"What about Nicky? Now that he got Dad's inheritance."

Ang's eyes turned sharp and black. "Nicky doesn't care. He's too stupid, just like Dad was," he sneered. "They aren't gonna take us out, Rose. I'm makin' sure of it. No more of this sick slavery. We're getting back our honor again."

"What?" I winced. They. They. They. All I ever heard was that nebulous they—referring to the bad guys, whoever they were. Everybody seemed to have their own.

Just then, Mugga pulled up in his Ford, the one that had a crack the shape of the profile of Mickey Mouse, straight down the windshield. Angelo traipsed off the porch and opened the passenger-side door.

"I won't tell." He winked, then ducked into the car, and they drove off.

I sat on the porch for a long time. Grandma and Popi never came out. I sat there so long that the mill workers slowly dwindled and left the street bare. Then one or two cars inched forward the other way on the street. I watched the midnight-shifters return to their sleeping houses.

Dad wasn't among them. I thought I saw him once, but it turned out to be that sick bastard Nico Gizzi. Somehow I managed to believe that I was going to hear Dad's clunky steel-toed boots knocking on the porch.

I found death difficult to agree with. The scent of Dad preserved some kind of presence that never quite died. It just changed, that's all. Absence was just a new kind of presence.

News got out—about Dad. I realized that when Charlotte came peddling down the street, and the look on her face told me she was there in hopes of comforting me.

"There's only one Nicky on this street," I told her.

"Huh?" Char looked at me, confused, but patronizingly endeared.

"Nicky Alex, the Syrian, is the only one here now. And I haven't even seen him in a while."

"Yeah, I guess you're right."

"There used to be three."

"But, pretty soon there won't be one anymore. When your brother gets home you'll be back up to two."

I shook my head. "He's not coming back." The words slipped from the quiet part of my brain.

"Rosie! What do you mean?"

"He's just not coming. I know it."

"You can't say that, Rose. You don't know."

"Well, you don't know that he is coming back!" I insisted.

"You're right, but I really believe he will." She patted my shoulder. "You've got to have a bit of faith."

Just then, Grandma came through the open front door, and her presence kept me from an annoyed rage. Her sturdy shoes clattered against the porch wood.

"Char-oletta, you stay for dinner?" She spoke to my friend with a kind voice and soft smile.

"I . . . ah—" Char didn't really have time to respond before my grandmother interrupted.

"You stay for dinner." Period.

And that was that. Grandma patted her on the back and returned into the house. From my starfish position on the floor, I could see in the front window, which normally glared a reverse picture of Elm Street. This time it reflected clouds, but I could see through their wispy waves into living room.

"Here comes Rooster!" Char announced. I looked over to the street and watched Popi hobble down the sidewalk. His chin sunk down and the top of his back curled in, as if he was a still-shot of someone who got punched in the chest. As he grew closer, I could see the tear stains or sweat stains around his collar. He didn't say anything. He barely looked up as he climbed the stairs and entered the house. Char kept her eyes fixed out on the street.

"Must be hard on them," I commented. "Ya know?" I rolled onto my stomach. "I mean, Popi just went down to the prison, to tell Nicky about Dad . . . There's just death everywhere. Nicky's been picked up for killin' somebody, and Dad got killed by his own heart . . . They've just seen a lot, ya know?"

"Yeah."

I shifted up onto my side, facing Char, who was in Dad's chair.

"Suppose you had to do it. Watch your kids die, family be lied about, and business go under," I continued.

Char looked reflective. "Yea. I don't know how they do it."

"Char, I ought-a tell you something."

"What's that?" Her soft eyes looked down on me, my heart went racing.

"I heard the radio before you got here this afternoon . . . Grandma went out to get some stuff from Hyde's, and so I turned it on, just to see, ya know . . . Grandma forbid me from TV and radio for a while until things calm down. She thinks that knowing all the ins and outs of this stuff is too much for me I think."

Char sighed a moan of acknowledgement.

"The Covert case is under some new considerations," I said. I had heard it on the news and my head spun, even though the Polariod that hid between the baseball cards was clear and evident. I still second-guessed the sight. And I was too horrified to look again. Logic evaded me, cause I couldn't handle it anymore.

"Really?"

I bit my lower lip. "Yeah." "They've been looking into Dad's death, apparently."

"And what does that have to due with Covert?" Char asked impatiently. She slid off the chair and onto the ground beside me. Her eyes demanded an answer. I couldn't voice what they found wedged between a rock and tree in the flooded Mahoning.

I lowered my voice. "Dad's the new suspect."

"What? Are you serious?" She burst out entirely too loudly.

I slapped my hand up against her mouth. "Char!" I whispered, with great breathy intensity.

She resumed in a more ethereal decibel, "How could they?"

"Well, ya know, I just remembered a talk I had with Angelo the other day. Apparently his boxing coach dropped him, because of somethin' Dad did.

"Rosie! How can you believe this? Char asked in a thunderous whisper. "There is no way that's true. Rosie!"

"I don't know. It just seems to be all lining up, ya know?"

Char's hands leapt onto the ground and grabbed the tops of my shoulders. Her fingers sunk into my back like a dog bite. "Rosie! Wake up!" She screamed.

I've never heard Charlotte yell like that before. Her fury pierced me. She pushed me off balance, and I braced myself catching my torso before I landing on my back.

When Grandma emerged onto the porch, Char spun around. "Sorry Mrs. Luce, we were just playing around," she said.

"You-a sure?" Grandma looked quizzically at us. I suppose her motherly ears identified the lack of veracity in the statement.

"Yeah, it's alright," Char answered.

Grandma puckered together the horizon of her lips and nodded. She turned back around and inched her way back into the house. Her footsteps creaked along, off into the distance.

"Rosie, I'm sorry," Char insisted.

I looked back at her, still jolted by her mere presence.

"Rose, I'm just sayin' Nicky or your Dad, or both or whatever, neither of them did this. They are good guys. I know them. I see how they love you all. Your Dad gets a little fired up sometimes, and sometimes he makes mistakes, but I don't think he'd ever come to a mistake this big, right?"

"Yeah," I quietly moaned.

"Nicky—he's quiet and has a mischievous look about him. He's just easy to blame, am I right? He's just easy to pick on. I don't think Nicky could ever harm somebody."

Just then I caught a glimpse of a few drip stains of blood on the legs of Dad's chair. Grandma and I had scrubbed the porch, but not the chair. My vision glued itself to them, hypnotized by the memory.

"You can't figure it all out," Char said, kindly. "You are just never going to figure it all out." She paused for a moment, and my eyes remained still fixed on the blood stains.

"The other day I finished *Huckleberry Finn*, and it was kind of nice to be done," she told me. "But, then it occurred to me—that it was not very much like life. You know what I mean?" She took hold of my forearm.

Slightly alarmed, I looked to her face.

"Rosie, I realized that life is not like most of the books I read. They all have endings. And I get to know what the ending is, and I get to make sense of the whole book, even read it again if I want. But life isn't like that. We don't get to know the ending. And when it happens to us, the end, we don't get to see what everything meant."

I could barely see her through the tears that welled in my eyes. "What do we do then?" I asked.

"We do what's right," she answered. "My mom says that to me every day. *Smile, please God, and do what's right.* You know, you can't control what other people do or how they respond. You are only in charge of yourself."

The watery glaze on my eyeball collected a rainbow of light. A tear escaped from my right eye and landed on Charlotte's arm. Another tear fell from my left eye onto my own arm. We studied those two tears, which appeared to have cosmic significance. They were more than tears. They were both mine, but Char had one and I had the other. For once, my soul was drenched in straight-shooting truth. The leaves rustled in the wind.

I don't think I ever cried as much in my whole life as I did after that sensation. All kinds of sadness and hope came out in salty drips. Char hugged me and held me and patted my head.

I think that is when I realized that Charlotte was my friend. A friend in a different way than just someone you spend time with and do wild things with or even just aren't repulsed by being around. She had a part of me. Perhaps she was sentimental and grossly patronizing, but I did love her in a way, and I knew that she loved me too, whatever her motivations. And though she barely realized the internal workings of my brain, she had a tear of mine. She's had it all along.

Piccolo's somber voice followed the breeze, weaving between our black shod bodies. Dad's funeral was a small affair. Me, Popi, Grandma and Ang had to stand in the front and toss dirt into the big hole where they dropped Dad. I mean they really did drop him. I guess when lowering him, the ropes slipped, and his boxed body slammed down. The small gathering jumped at the crack, but nobody said anything. They just awkwardly carried on as normal.

Before the ceremony and the whole dropping scandal, Hog brushed up against my right arm. He said he came to support me, whatever that means. I didn't need any support as far as I could tell. He thought he'd comfort me by letting me know a "little something." He went on and on about how Dad's death wasn't fair. I only listened to half of his seven-minute monologue in which he expressed his great concern over the corruption of our city's social structures. The part I did catch, though, was his rather strong assertion that the police had picked off Dad and covered it up by the report of the heart attack. He said the police controlled everything, because the city municipalities had control of them, and if all the Italian brothers wanted to keep their godforsaken jobs and their dignity, the brothers have to join together.

"Eventually," Hog continued, "they'll put an end to us." Hog kept going on about our "uprising," but I didn't know what he was talking about, and I didn't care. I had no good reason to trust a hoodlum. Then he paused for a moment. He leaned close to my ear. "I know about Angelo."

I swung my head around and glared at him, face to face.

He raised his eyebrows and slapped one hand on my shoulder. "We're real proud of 'm."

At that precise moment, like a period to the sentence, the grave wardens had dropped the box. I shuddered, but Piccolo's somber voice waved on with the breeze.

After the ceremony concluded, people still hung around, wandering around the Italiano graveyard, paying respects to their own. Most of the neighbors who came showed up just for good measure and respect for Popi and Grandma. They all assumed Dad was a murderer, I was certain of it. Luckily, for once it was acceptable for me to avoid eye contact and just be seen as mourning and embarrassed and not just rude.

I stood with Grandma, who still peered into the hole. Officer Deleone came up from behind us. He shook Popi's hand and explained his serious sorrow over the whole affair. Just past Deleone's, bulbous hair, I caught a glimpse of Angelo. In the distance he leaned against a tree and glared across at Deleone. Ang's eyes followed Deleone from the moment of the shake through the departure of his car. Deleone gave a glance to Angelo, but I noticed he didn't bother going over to him. I mean, he didn't talk to me either, but I supposed this had something to do with what Hog, that bastard, said.

Ang's face still looked yellowy and slick, kind of like our laminate kitchen table. He and Mugga got straight-up plastered the night before. I knew that because when the sun had set, the house was quiet, and I was going out to get the coffee cup I'd left on the front porch. I heard Mugga's car putting along down Elm. He shifted into park. I suppose neither of them could see me. The shadows of the porch hid me. I sunk back against the chilled siding. It took at least five minutes for Ang to get out of the car, but when he did, I swear I could smell that sour mist waft clear across the yard. The assortment of liquor fuming out of that car could wake a man in his grave. He flung the car door shut and stumbled up the walkway, his feet lazily whipping around. He didn't make it very far, and he ended up collapsing in the front yard. I wasn't too alarmed. I had seen this kind of thing plenty of times. After Mugga chugged off, I emerged from my shadow to inspect the specimen deposited in the yard. The alcohol had knocked him out cold. For a moment I considered using Dad's beloved red creeper to wheel him around back, just so he wouldn't cause us any neighborhood commotion when the sun rose. I had just risen to my feet when Ang tossed a little and woke up. I could see, even by the light of the moon, his contorted face, yellowy and slick. I left him there and went back to my own business.

Later, in the kitchen, I poured myself some water before heading up to bed. Then I saw a little flicker out in the back alley. Ang had finally moved from his headlong location for a backstage midnight smoke. I drank my water and gave him some time to sober up before I checked on him. He wasn't at all startled or angry when I came out the back door, probably due to the liquor, to be honest. He lit my cigarette when I sat on the stoop next to him.

"Nev'err thought it'd be like'is," he stammered.

I remained silent.

"Nev'err thought me."

"Never thought what about ya?" I asked.

"Nev'err thought I'd be takin' over," he continued, "ya know. We live in hell, ya know. Can't fix anything . . . da'boy's r'out f'r us, an the law got us in the stocks. Takin' everything. Everybody go'ot som'thin with the Luce's." He swirled his hand in the air waving like the queen of England. "We gotta get right with da'boys. We owe'm big time. We gotta pay'm, give'm at money. Get back in d'biz, ya know. Dis time I'll real-ly do it. Make'us straight."

I kept my horrid thoughts to myself, but I couldn't keep them from myself. The alley caged us both in. I realized we weren't going anywhere. At last the truth was coming out, and all those suspicions about us were proving true.

Some clouds floated in, fogging the moonlight. A coyote howled from beyond the river, echoing through the quiet pit we called home.

All of my suspicions were confirmed. I knew we had bad blood. Once I allowed myself to see that, though, I felt an odd sense of freedom. Deep down, I had known there was something wretched in me. To my great delight, my family wasn't cursed after all. We just had bad blood. Had it all along. I was relieved to find out that I wasn't the cause of all this hunting and hiding. It's just what's due to us.

I watched Angelo puff out a thick wind.

"I just gotta . . . get . . . dem da' cash, but I know how." His hair had grown out quite a bit. If it hadn't been wavy, it would have nearly brushed his shoulders. A month earlier, I wouldn't have recognized him with that grimy hair and the yellowy gleam on his face, smothered in cigarette smoke and reeking of half-digested alcohol. Never would-a guessed it.

I leaned my head up against the back door and stretched out my legs. Ang did the same. He slipped his arm behind my back and pulled me in to his side.

"Gonna save us, Rosie, make'r wrongs right, don't you worry."

It felt good to have his arm around me again.

"I know you killed Covert, Ang." I yawned. "Saw you kill 'm, suck that blood right out of 'm. Just wanted you to know." I puffed another gray cloud. "I won't tell."

I had expected Angelo to respond, but he didn't. When I sat up, I could see that his head had been resting against the sill, and he was out cold again and didn't know if he heard me or not. I smothered my jack and left him there.

I reckon he slept out back most of the night, because I heard some rumbling around just before dawn. When he emerged from his room, he was showered and readied for the funeral.

He kept quiet all morning. And I don't mean he didn't talk. I mean his body said absolutely nothing. It was nearly irreverent. So I didn't bother trying to talk to him. Being in the light of day, I could tell he went back to disregarding me. None of that drunk sentimentality lingered in his system.

Father Piccolo stepped between Grandma and me. He reached around both of us and redundantly expressed his vague sorrow. Grandma gave him a little knowing smile and patted him on the back before she walked off to Angelo. Piccolo bent down to me.

I suppose closure has a therapeutic aftertaste. After putting Dad in the hole, covering him up and leaving him, it really did feel like the end. When I would think of Dad, I'd see him sleeping in that box, lying in that hole.

I slept really well that night—never moved, straight on my back. I woke up with my hands folded on my chest. Though the crucifix had departed some time earlier, I still kept the habit of falling asleep with one hand on my chest. I woke up just like that.

The dawn peeked into my window, filling the room with that tranquil, familiar blue. Hog's words replayed over and over in my mind. "Real proud," they are "real proud" of Ang. Real proud. Real proud. The tick of my watch echoed around in the drawer next to my bed. Real proud. Real proud. I slipped out of the covers and wobbled across to my closet. The little cardboard box had collected some dust over the weeks. The dust kept a tight hold on the lid, even as I plucked it off. Grandma's Swinger sat in there like a dust-covered toy under a couch. It sat next to those stacks of worn baseball cards and the Super ball. I lifted up the baseball cards and pulled out the collection of Polaroids. The one of Ang was on top. I kicked the box back into the closet and carried the photo back over to my bed.

The photo was grainy, and a dark undeveloped smudge blotted out the one man's face, but Ang was bright and clear—long slender knife at his side, head turned, looking over his shoulder to that sound in the distance. He looked frightened.

I placed the photo in the drawer with my watch and made my way downstairs. Before I headed to the porch I stirred up some coffee. The brisk air fluttered the curtains covering the kitchen window. Dad's leather jacket hung in the hall closet limp and lost. I removed it from his wiry hanger and slipped my arms into the Dad-shaped form.

I sneaked out the door and closed it gently, and with free outdoor-pomp I plopped onto Dad's chair. The zipper of the fully zipped-up coat poked up into my neck, so I rolled it down, allowing my air passageway to be cleared of the obstacle. I also felt the square edge of a little cardboard box jab in between my ribs. I retrieved the pack of cigarettes Dad had left in that secret pocket of his coat. Half the pack was already smoked. I figured Dad smoked a few while he walked out to the traps that morning.

I lit up a jack and let the smoke cascade over my face. The first tears have the most trouble getting out, but after that they seem to just follow in easy order. I let the salty little streams run down my face, puddling on my t-shirt beneath the leathery layers, hidden from even me except for my collar's cool, clingy wetness. Eyes shut, I rested my head against the chilly paneling.

That's when I felt her.

She was stroking my hair like she used to when I was a little girl. She didn't alarm me, it was like she was supposed to be there, like she'd been there all along. I kept my eyes shut and let her stroke my head. She spoke. She said that it was going to be alright. She said I didn't have to worry, that he was in a good place now—with her. And one day we'd be all together. She said I was strong and wise, just like Dad. And she said that I could be sad, but I didn't have to be afraid. It was all going to be all right.

A ravenous blue jay squawked in the front yard. My eyes involuntarily winged open. She drifted away with the faded smoke.

I thought about Nicky sitting in that prison cell. I wondered if he was alone, or if it was one of those shared cells, and if he had a bed or he lay on one of those wooden benches. Hog informed me about all of the possibilities and varieties of jail cells.

Nicky missed the funeral, but it was probably better for all of us. He and Angelo were having quite a time. They always were at odds. I mean, their personalities were blatantly opposed to one another. But the heat of those past few weeks really ignited a fire that I wasn't sure would ever end. Yes, sure, they fought over pie and laughed at dinner, reminiscing about the old stories, but most of the grand tension, even in their silence, tightened the house like a guitar string out of tune and ready to snap. Nicky was the favorite and the honored one, but Angelo was the respectable one, the one that really cared about us. I guess Angelo just had enough. I took to setting my ear against their door late at night. Ang did all the talking. He was so perplexed by Nicky's apathetic reaction to "everything." Everybody developed this way of talking about everything by talking about nothing. When Angelo set his mind on something, his heart went with it. Every decision, every action, every word was severe. He was just a very excessive person.

Dingding. Dingding. Hog came peddling through the yard. That was the first time I actually saw the kid on a bicycle, and it was a strange sight indeed, like a little tub of honey zooming about.

"Hey Rose!" he shouted as he wrecked into the front stairs.

"What in the name of Jimmy Davis are ya doin' here at this hour?"

"I . . ." He crawled up the stair and scurried to the swing. "I . . . just couldn't wait to tell you."

"Good God, stop yelling! Everybody's sleepin' around here," I insisted.

"Listen here," he whispered. "Boy, oh, boy you gonna be happy."

"Well go ahead and get on with it!"

"Nicky's gettin' out-a the slammer. Heard it at the Joint yesterday."

"Oh yeah? You trust them damn *ragazzi*?" I sneered.

"Yeah, I do. Always been right, far as I can 'member."

A train chugged in the distance, and its horn billowed in that crisp breeze. Hog's head flung to the side. He stood up.

"Mmm. Welp." Still looking away. "Better get goin.'"

"Got somewhere to be?"

Hog pranced down the stairs. "Sure thing."

And just like that, he was off down the alley across Elm, peddling his wobbly bike out of sight.

I supposed Dad killed that guy after all—according to the state. You know, despite Officer Steve Subdolo's gargantuan and ridiculous shoes, I thought him to be pretty level-headed and incapable of such ternary. Not that he was in charge or anything, but his Pittsburgh accent made him sound respectable in the least. But, to tell you the truth, I was kind of happy

Dad was the one acquitted. He didn't have the chance to defend himself, and that, that indeed was a blessing.

Soon enough Popi emerged from the house. I had changed into work-wear and snagged some bread and cheese. We were off to the shop. The sun shot rays down through the tree limbs which mingled with the telephone pole shadows. I did expect those telephone poles to come alive sometimes. Especially suspected it when I cycled down the alleys by myself. I thought for sure they'd rip themselves from their electric tethers and with stomping booms wreck Mahoningtown like Godzilla. Unfortunately, I'd witness it all and be left, the lone survivor.

The man with the stogie nodded to Popi. Two curly headed women waved out their windows. Everything was finally back to normal. Though I was very surprised at the fact that these people still liked us and all. Seemed like it just took Dad getting picked off for them to respect us again. Dad died for a noble cause after all.

I was glad to have the shock and the funeral behind us. All the black and the mums and the gloom. All the digging and dirt. Dad looked kind of alive in his casket. Grandma had him put in his favorite suit. The navy-blue one with the white shirt, two buttons opened. He looked sharp. I think he even breathed once. I liked looking at him. He looked really relaxed. It was nice to see him like that, and he even had a little smirk. That's the only part of the funeral I liked. I got to look at Dad between guests and family and friends coming to hug us. Me and Father Piccolo would go and look at Dad together.

Father Piccolo got down on his knee and looked me in the face. He said that Dad was a very good man, the best that he had known, and that I shouldn't think any less than that when I thought of him. Father Piccolo's eyes shot lightning. A bright sincerity struck me deep in the heart.

Father Piccolo mentioned "the resurrection" that day when he had his speech. I can't remember much of what he said, but I do remember that he said that one day we would all be resurrected and live together on the new earth with new bodies. I wondered if that's what Hog told me about, the *uprising*. During that resurrection talk something got caught somewhere under my blackening ribs. I remember thinking it was like a bit of light that made my whole body feel good, alive. Afterward, I asked Father Piccolo about this sensation. He said it was called hope. As Grandma and I rolled the meatballs, I still felt the hope.

Like I said, Nicky couldn't come to the funeral because they still had him locked up. I hadn't seen him for like a week. I never went to visit him— figured he wouldn't care to see me. I wanted to bring that up with Grandma, but it was such a peaceful moment. I couldn't risk it.

"Ech ehmehm," Grandma cleared her throat. "I think was-a good Nicky not at funeral," she said. That surprised me. She explained: "Its-a been too many pressure on-a him. The old men would-a tell him things. Maybe tell-a him that he gotta get him together and take-a care of us." She clicked her tongue. I kept at the meatballs. "He just might-a felt bad. You know-a when my papa die in old country, my brother run away. He ashame'ed the whole family. But Nicky he would-a not do-a that. He-a just suck it all in and . . ." Her arms comically formed a bigger and bigger circle in front of her. "Poof. He become-a Popi!"

I laughed at the idea of Nicky becoming an old, serious, quiet shoe-maker, but I think I understood it too.

The front door opened and shut under the soft melodies of Sir Cole. I could hear Angelo's dancing steps prancing down the hallway. He swung around the corner and into the kitchen, a smile strewn across his face.

"My two favorite women!" He bent down to kiss Grandma at her temple and came over to me to wrap is lanky arms around my head.

"Erremmmnnn!" I voiced a muffled scream and pulled his arm down a hair width. "I can't breathe!"

Laughing, he let his arms fall away and ducked around the corner of the doorway.

Grandma and I exchanged smirks and got back to rolling our meat-balls. The record player screeched to a halt and, shortly thereafter, it started another sizzling spin. The setting sunlight beamed in the window and cast even sharper shadows across the table.

Angelo didn't come back into the kitchen. I imagined after he flipped the record he'd just laid down on the couch and listened. Grandma took some bowls and spoons from the table and set them in the sink. Her hands snatched the full tray of meatballs and slipped them into the oven. I felt a wave of heat splash against my back, but I kept working away on the meat that was left. My tray was about three-fourths full and probably wouldn't fill-up completely.

Grandma's butt swayed ever so slightly to the music. Before I knew it, I swayed a little, too, and pretty soon I was bobbing my head and roll-ing meatballs to the beat. Grandma had stopped her washing and just swayed—looking out the back window. Her shadow moved about the back wall where a painting, the rolling hills of Tuscany hung. Nicky had painted that in art class the previous year. I think Art was the only class he went to in those days.

That cool velvety voice rippled through that thick air. I couldn't help but smile. A darting shadow caught the corner of my eye, and Angelo came bounding into the kitchen. He grabbed Grandma's hands and started to dance.

They laughed and danced. The setting sun twinkled across their eyes. The aroma of roasting garlic cascaded down off the heat waves that rose from the oven and rushed past Grandma and Angelo, who started to sing. I raised my raw-meated and egg-whited hands, shut my eyes, and swayed them in the air.

Down the hall, the front door rattled. Angelo backed away, still dancing, through the kitchen doorway. Grandma followed him into the hallway. And by the time I stuck my head around the corner Angelo was opening the door.

The prodigal son had returned.

Instead of the long embrace I expected, Nicky blazed right in and knocked Angelo straight to the floor. Bewildered, Grandma stood still and silent. But I surged up from my chair and stormed down the hall.

"NICKY!" I shouted. "What the hell?"

My knees crashed against the floor next to Angelo. I bent down close to his face. His eyes flickered. Once he came to full-consciousness, he shoved me over into the wall and struggled to his feet. Before Ang got straight, Nicky grabbed his shirt and threw him back into the wall—bearing his forearm into Ang's chest.

"Tell me right now!" Nicky screamed. "Tell me you're not in on Mugga's damned trucking business!"

"Get off me!" Ang wrestled Nicky's grasp, but couldn't combat Nicky's thick weight.

"Angelo," Nicky growled.

Ang broke an arm free and plowed his hand into Nicky's face. I lunged back to crawl away. They twirled across the hall. This time Nicky landed, pinned against the opposite wall.

From beneath Ang's weight, Nicky moaned. "I knew you been doin' jobs for them. But, don't tell me this."

Ang scowled. "I'm not your little pet to keep track of!"

"You gonna get us all killed."

Angelo slapped Nicky in the face.

Nicky took a moment to recover. When his sunken head lifted back up, he continued undeterred. "Pick us off one at a time."

"Are you sayin' its my fault—Dad gettin' picked off?" Angelo screamed.

Nicky stomped his foot on top of Ang's and threw him back onto the floor.

"Dad was a gidrul'!" Ang screamed. "Is that it? Is that what you want me to say? Dad was a damned gidrul'?"

Nicky stood up straight, towering over Angelo. Ang looked like a crinkled up paper on the floor. But his voice was still strong. "Dad deserted the best thing that ever happened to us. Turned his back on the family. We had no one in this country, and you know as well as me the law hates Italiano, wants us dead and gone ever since we got here."

Nicky remained standing, looking down with the fire of damnation in his eyes.

Ang shook his head. "Dad's who got us into this shit, and you know it. If we're gonna survive, we gotta get things right with the brothers."

At that statement, my body temperature rose. Blood pumped and thumped in my ears. I hated Angelo right then. He had the *malocchio after-all*—I knew it. When I'd get sick Grandma would ward away the *malocchio*, or the *malooch* as she called it. She'd drop oil in boiling water and then make me say Hail Mary's. The sicknesses would more or less evaporate within minutes. But, this seemed to be a different *malocchio* a bigger, darker, holier one. And we all had bad blood from birth, seeds of evil waiting in our veins, except maybe Grandma, since she married into the Luce blood. But this dark fury was different. Ang used to be the life of the family, sincere. But I'd seen that sudden, dark fury arise too many times. The sickness could only be the *malocchio* taking over him—awaking the blood of our veins.

"Oh-h-h. You want charge of this family, don't you? Want to prove to us that Dad was wrong for neglecting you." Nicky crept forward. "You don't want to be *me* anymore. You think you're *better* than me, huh? Think you deserve the honor?" Nicky bent over, nearing Angelo's face, and with the bitter fury of a thousand wolves screamed, "*Well, you can fucking have it!*"

Angelo jacked him right in the left eye.

As Nicky fell onto his knees, he grabbed Angelo around the neck and plowed his head down onto those old wooden floorboards.

Angelo would never admit to the *malocchio*. He clearly didn't know what seized him. No Lord's Prayer, no hail Mary's, could save him.

Just then, Popi smashed through the door. That door hit the wall so hard that the family photos crashed to the living room floor. Nicky's hand squeezed around Angelo's throat.

CHAPTER 16

I made up my mind. The only way to get the *malocchio* out of him would be to kill the one that cursed him.

I heard a *click-click.*

"Yous about to kill a *made man*, Nick." Popi pressed a pistol into Nicky's ear. Immediately, Nicky's hands dropped to the floor. To this day, Angelo's raspy gasp still rings in my head. Still holding the gun to Nicky's head, Popi tugged on the collar of his shirt and led him up from the ground onto his feet. Popi tucked his hand into his suit jacket pocket and pulled out a white envelope. He tossed it over to Ang, who still lay on the floor.

Popi continued, "You wanna stay-a civilian bambino? No touch him again!" He let down the gun and proceeded to walk down the hall to the kitchen. Nicky turned to the door, while Angelo rose. Seemingly oblivious to the envelope, he climbed the stairs to his room.

That white letter lay in the hallway with me—the only remaining human. Its stubby form had landed face up, and I saw that it was blank. I stretched over to pick it up. I stretched to snag one of the corners between my fingers. It wasn't very smooth dragging, as an envelope ought to be. I flipped it over to reveal a waxy, red seal on the underside. Unlike that envelope I had found in the door crack sometime before, this seal was already broken. Since Angelo hadn't read it, I supposed that Popi must have opened it.

Some floorboards creaked in the kitchen. Not wanting to be seen snooping, I shoved the envelope into my pocket and hopped up to my feet. Popi, cigar in hand, crossed the hallway into the living room. Grandma hated when he smoked inside, since she spent most of her time scrubbing, dusting, wiping, and sweeping. Clean spaces were her pride, but what could she actually have done about Popi? Perhaps, I thought, maybe she secretly liked when the boys wrecked the house because it gave her something meaningful to do.

I waltzed out the front door and to the alley behind the house. Air gently swept down the quiet strip of gravel. The birds had already gone home for the night, but a lone cricket played its tune. I plopped onto the cement step and slipped the letter out of the envelope. It was addressed to "Boxer." It did seem kind of risky to put an actual name on such a secret artifact. But I guess that didn't matter any more for Ang. Popi did say he was a made-man now. When I was a kid, I asked Popi, why he and Dad had to go to meet-ups all the time, and why I couldn't come. He told me it was because they were made-men. I had not the slightest clue what that meant, but fortunately one time Popi had some wine in his system and a cigar in his mouth—his most delightful kind of time. So he disclosed that those men in suits had our backs as long as he and Dad had theirs.

"Like family?" I asked.

"Like family."

I suddenly dreamed that one day I could be a made-man too.

It occurred to me then that maybe this was the freedom that Angelo always wanted, the "unstuckness" he often talked about, the loosening of the trap. Popi wore suits and the gold chain, and I supposed Angelo would begin to do the same. Honestly, I kind of wished I'd kept that crucifix—couldn't remember why I turned it over to the church in the first place. I flipped open the letter.

Got a contract on Carmidio, need a driver, meet me at midnight, Hyde's. I'll bring the truck. —M. A shiver sped down my spine. "M" for Moon, I thought. That son of a bitch. I knew from the first time I saw him, with that thick scar around his neck, with the crucifix and no *cornetto* or *mano corno*. Stealing from the nun proved it. He bore the *malocchio* too.

Suddenly, I heard Grandma shriek. My hearted raced as I quickly folded the letter and envelope, stuffed them into my shoe, under my foot, and leapt up into the house. Grandma was standing at the top of the basement stairs, and Angelo had already bounded down from his bedroom. He leapt onto the floor, grabbed Grandma from behind the back, and slapped his hand over her mouth.

Popi's lazy voice resonated from the living room, "Told-a you not-a go down there." His feet stayed propped up on the coffee table, and his disheveled newspaper remained in hand.

I lurched my head around the basement doorway. Angelo lunged around Grandma toward me. His hand palmed my face and flung it backward. The whiplash disoriented me enough that I twirled around trying to find my balance, but I landed at the corner of the wall and floor. Nevertheless, it was too late. I had already seen the man at the bottom of the basement stairs. A rope tied up his hands and feet, preventing him from getting out of the trough of brown lumpy liquid that he was dumped in. Oddly enough, his mouth wasn't taped, yet he didn't make a peep, just white eyes peering up.

Angelo reached down and grabbed my face. "Learn to listen!" he growled.

I stared up into his fire-blazing eyes. I saw a hole, a deep black hole funneling straight into his darkened soul. Somebody had to save him before he spread it to us all, before he ruined all of us.

I sprung up and lurched out the back door. The sun weighed heavily on the horizon, peaking through the thick trees. I hopped on my bike. No breeze fought my ride. The leaves remained silent, unchanging, unwavering, drooping and overturned, waiting for rain. The darkening sky chased me down Cascade as I headed for the sun. I knew I had to move fast if I was going to make it back before the storm.

I saw Father Piccolo locking the final latch on the church doors as I dumped my bike next to the flower bed. "Father!" I trampled over to those cement, church stairs.

"Rosie. So sorry. I've just locked up for the evening."

"No, no . . ."

He interrupted me, "Perhaps, tomorrow?"

"No, didn't come to pray."

He looked at me with furrowed brows.

"You got to help me!" I insisted. "Please." I heard my own voice waver as the word "please" escaped my stubborn lips.

"What is it child?"

"Somethin' bad is gonna happen, but you see," my puffing lungs breathed out. "I can't do anything about it. Can you help me?"

"What is it? I'll help in any way I can."

I slipped the note into the pocket of his jacket. "Take this to someone that can stop it."

He reached for his pocket, but I blocked his hand, before he got there. "Wait till I'm gone."

He looked alarmed. "Rosie, I hope everything is all right."

I like to think I was out of sight, before he could ask any questions, or minimize his ability to help. But honestly, I think he probably just voluntarily kept speechless and let me go on my way.

The storm held off until I made it all the way to bed, but I didn't even get to sleep before the wind-thrown rain crashed against my window. It thudded and thundered for about two hours before it calmed to a hiss. I wondered if it woke Dad up, but I caught myself before I remembered that Dad wasn't down stairs, lying on his back on that pull-out bed. Instead, I just pretended that he was down there. He had gotten up to get some water and now he was sleeping just fine.

When the clouds parted, I heard wet steps beneath my window. Without hesitation I flung back my covers and tip-toed over. Indeed, a dark figure lurked beneath the window. It moved across the yard approaching the back of the house. I felt my jaw tighten and my shoulders rise. I could only imagine that it was Moon down there waiting for Angelo.

I squeezed out my cracked-open bedroom door and snuck down the stairs, avoiding every squeak. I knew that this time a squeak would be disastrous. It would take only one noise to wake somebody or stop Moon in his tracks or, worst, even wake Angelo.

At the bottom of the stairs, I crawled across the hallway floor until I reached the kitchen stove. As my eyes transcended the window sill, I laid my gaze on the suited dark man who paced across the wet gravel. He turned back toward me. I ducked, plunking my head between the burners.

He stayed out there for at least ten minutes and then left. Piccolo—I wondered if he had done what I asked. I still didn't know if I could trust him. But what's the worst that could happen? I asked myself. Even if I threw the letter in the fire, I had already done the work of keeping Ang from another crime, and I suppose that was a victory in itself. But I had strong sense that Moon had started this black plague, infecting us all with the virus that awoke our true blood. It didn't even matter if Moon deserved to die. I hoped that if he did die, we might be made good again.

The floor tile was cold on my bare skin. When I was a kid, Grandma and I used to lie flat on the tile all the time. In the summertime heat, the tile felt cool, refreshing. I guess when her knees got bad, we stopped. I don't even remember when that was. I guess it just kind of drifted away with all those other childhood practices.

One time we were resting on the tile, lying on our stomachs. Then the floor started to quake, but I didn't notice until after the walls started to creak. Grandma jumped up and dragged me out the back door. It was one of those rare Pennsylvania earthquakes. Haven't felt one since.

A sound yanked my thoughts back to the present. The sudden shriek of a siren blasted through the humid air. At the sound I realized that everyone, and I mean the whole neighborhood would wake up. I bolted to the stairs and bounded up with silent haste. I had just slid into my bedroom when I heard Nicky's and Angelo's doors creak open. I opened my door, too.

Angelo swooped down the stairs. Popi came hobbling after him. Nicky and I followed them out onto the front porch. Three cop cars surrounded Hyde's drug store. Six policeman stood outside, guns in hand, three facing the store and three facing the street. Soon enough a couple cops dragged a suited guy out through the front door. A stream of blood trickled off his right hand.

I was afraid to ask, but curiosity overcame me. "Who is it?"

Nobody answered. Ang, Nicky and Popi streamed one-by-one back into the house. But my feet stayed planted. An ambulance screeched to a halt, and Steve Subdolo staggered out the door of Hyde's and across its shiny threshold supporting a wounded Carmine. Subdolo walked him to the ambulance, past another cop who cuffed the suited guy and led him around one of the cars. The man in the suit looked up, and stared right at me—into my own eyes.

I was wrong. It wasn't Moon. It was Mugga.

I was stuck, cemented to the porch, caught in some horrible trance. A hand touched my shoulder. I turned to see Grandma's knowing and gentle eyes gazing down at me.

"*Vieni dentro*" she urged, motioning me inside. Nothing to see.

I looked back over my shoulder as she guided me back to the door. There was something to see. I had made a terrible, terrible mistake.

Later on that day, Char called. She told me that her Mom wouldn't allow her to come down to Mahoningtown anymore. So I was left to ride the line alone that day.

After all the peddling my mind began to settle. The slimy nightcrawler-infested road sizzled under my tires. It was good to get all of that stored up anger and fear out of my system.

I hopped in the back door. Grandma had Nat playing. The tip of her feather duster fluffed out from the living room doorway. When I rounded the corner, to my surprise, I saw that the person wielding it was Popi. Odd, yes. That's a woman's job, and he was pretty adamant about that.

"Where's Grandma?"

"She take-a nap-a."

Grandma never took naps. "What're you doin'?"

"Clean."

I'm not sure what exactly had come over the man. He'd spent the last how many, like, sixty-odd years not laying a finger on a cleaning product.

The closest thing to cleaning that he ever cleaned was his rather obsessive habit of polishing shoes. It did make sense after all, shoes were his life.

He coughed—loudly. Then, sputtered out littler coughs.

The sound jolted my nerves. "You all right Popi?" I asked.

Nicky came in the door and kicked off his shoes at the entry. I was supposed to do that too, but the back door never had the same prestige as the front door, and so I often instinctually neglected making a habit of knocking them off back there.

Popi coughed again. "Just-a little dust," he pattered. The coughs came back. Then he lost his grip on the feather duster. Feathers and all, it flopped down hard, knocking his coffee cup off of the end table. His eyes seemed to roll back into his head.

My limbs shook a little. Nicky pushed me to the side and careened across the living room.

Accompanying a loud hack was the blood, spewing out from Popi onto the carpet. Grandma wasn't going to like that. I felt my chest tighten. Right as Nicky latched onto Popi's arm, Popi's head dropped and his knees buckled, but Nicky caught him under the armpits and lowered him to the ground.

I started to feel my own legs moving. Before I could think, I had launched out the front door and leaped off the porch. But right at that moment a cop car pulled up. The fuzz had been making rounds down round Mahoningtown ever since the incident the previous night. I had seen at least seven cars when I was riding the line earlier.

Officer Steve Subdolo peered out the driver's window as his car inched forward. "You okay?" he asked me.

I shook my head. I was largely unaware of what I looked like, but I felt my feet screech to a halt. Right in the middle of the road Subdolo shifted the car into park. The emergency brake gritted against the tires. He leaped out and hand-on-gun whirled around the front of the car.

"Popi," was the only word that I could get out.

Subdolo grabbed my shoulder. "Where?"

I nodded back toward the house.

Subdolo barreled down the sidewalk and up the porch steps. He didn't even stop at the door, like protocol. He just launched in. That's when I realized that I didn't know where I was going. I was running nowhere. I ignored my thoughts and turned back toward the house.

They ended up taking Popi to the hospital in Subdolo's car. I didn't go. Grandma woke up, but she didn't make it down the stairs before they took Popi out.

When Grandma stepped out on the porch, I was sitting alone out there on Dad's chair smoking a cigarette. She didn't say anything about the smoking. She just sat on the swing and swung in silence.

"They took Popi to the hospital," I said.

"Yes-a, I hear." Her eyes scanned the street. She didn't seem surprised or worried at all.

"Did you hear what happened?"

She looked out across the grass at the side walk and then up into the maple tree. "Yes, I hear," she said with stoic gaze. "He been-a sick for a while."

"Sick?" Why hadn't anyone told me? "How long?"

"Long."

"What?" I felt betrayed. "Why didn't you say anything?"

"No good to say-a."

"What do you mean? And what kind of sick?" *Malocchio*, I thought.

She still faced the maple tree. "Cancer in the lung."

Did everyone know but me. "Do the boys know?"

She shook her head up and down.

"Did Dad know?"

She nodded.

"Who else knows?"

"Only a few. Carmi—"

"What about Father Piccolo?" I interrupted.

"Yes, he know-a. Pray-a for heal."

Grandma turned to me. Tears welled up in her eyes. "Everyone has-a to die, Rosie. You can't-a stop it . . . Your dad, Popi, me, you—we all die-a." Her tears broke, parting into two gentle streams. "We know-a the end coming for Popi." She looked back out toward the street and back up to the top of the maple. The quivers in her voice flattened out. "We knew-a. So we prepare. It was-a good for him. And-a for me."

I looked at my feet and tossed the cigarette butt onto the porch. My foot smashed it in, grinding it down so it could be lifted by the wind. I bent down and picked up what was left and tossed it onto the ash tray. That smell drifted through the air. That smell used to make me sense Dad's presence. I think at some point I must have just grown fond of the smoking and forgotten about him. That made me ashamed. Talking about Popi's coming end brought the smell back. The fragrant-memory filled my lungs and found its way to my brain. I remembered. I remembered Dad sitting there, reading that Bible, smoking a cigarette. I remembered the way that Dad used to take his bread and sop up every speck of sauce, oil, and vinegar on his cleared plate. Nicky would try to convince Grandma that she didn't have to wash it. Remembered him yelling at me for torturing frogs on the sidewalk and remembered him yelling over to Carmine words I didn't understand. I remembered Carmine laughing and sweeping. I even remembered Angelo laying on the swing, reading a Spiderman comic while Dad drank coffee and kibitzed with Popi. I guess I had to make due with the fact that Popi would be a memory too, sooner rather than later.

Dad's spare cigarette rolled, in the breeze, across the stool. I caught it as it fell off the edge.

"Grandma? Why'd Dad always keep this extra cigarette sittin' here?" I placed it back on the stool.

A smile warmed her face. "He-a keep one there for a lo-o-o-o-ong time." She got a faraway look. "He keep it there since his brother go-a to war."

I still didn't understand.

"I think . . ." She nodded. "I think-a he waiting."

"Waiting for Uncle Johnny?"

Grandma nodded.

"I thought he died out there."

"No-a," the smile slipped off her face and weighed down her jaw. "No-a. Nobody find-a him . . . Lost."

Maybe they told me he died when I was younger because they knew I couldn't understand anything else, and I already understood death. Or maybe they just never wanted to tell me that my uncle might have been blasted into a million pieces out in some field. Or worse yet, that maybe he didn't *want* to come home.

"I-a worried about Angelo," Grandma interjected into my thoughts.

"Me, too," I said without thinking. I wondered if she might help me understand.

"Grandma?"

"Mm?" She raised her chin toward me while making eye contact that assured me I had her full attention.

"I . . . ah.. I . . . What's goin' on around here? Mahoningtown, I mean?" Although I really did want to look away, I maintained the eye contact.

"What you mean-a?"

"You know. . . . " I swept my hand out and motioned along Elm Street.

Grandma scooted herself back on the seat a bit. Her folded hands tightened, except for a tapping pointer finger. She breathed a big breath and exhaled slowly. Then she did it again. The sun was going down and lighting up the maple. Minor shafts of light beamed out the other side.

"Well-a," Grandma started. She shook her head. "I don't know." Then she said nothing.

I looked at her waiting for some sign of a white lie or a black lie. Some subtle eye movement that could communicate forced decency. But her eyes never folded, until she looked back to me.

"Popi, never tell-a me all. You-a see, it was-a bee'siness, and he never discuss-a bees'iness." Her hands relaxed and punctuated her words. "He good-a man, good-a father, good-a husband." Tears welded in her eyes again. "But every good-a man has-a secrets, you see. And, I always knew-a that Popi keep-a bees'iness to him." Her lips pressed a slim, straight line with slightly down turned edges. She tapped her head. "But, I-a knew, I-a knew." She nodded and looked down at the wooden deck. Her fingers tapped against the scraggly wooden swing.

I'm not real sure of what she saw in those floor slats, maybe a memory she wished she didn't remember. At any rate, whatever thought she had made her head snapped up. But when she looked back up to the treetop, her delicious smile broke through and so did a kind of laugh—the kind that's just a puff of air exiting the nose.

I wondered what "bees'iness" she meant. Reaching down for another cigarette, I asked, "What business? Like the shoe shop?"

"No-a. More."

My eye jutted up to see whether her "no" was answering my question or scolding me for the cigarette . . . or worst of all, both. Preemptively, I put the second cigarette back in the box.

"Sure, that-a shoe shop. But, also another bees'iness," She continued, "There is-a bees'iness, Italiano brothers, *familia* bess'iness that help-a all us. They not help-a us first. I no saw them—" She stopped and looked around, and I realized her voice had grown more hushed. "I no saw them. But-a one day they show up at-a back door for Popi."

"When was that?"

"It a . . . six month after we-a open shoe-a shop. We just-a move into this-a house from leetle apartment down street." She pointed down past Hyde's. Something seemed to snap inside her, and she quickly stood. "I think maybe we make-a dinner before boys get-a back."

That was the end of the conversation—the most intimate conversation I ever had with Grandma, and for sure the only serious one. I knew that when we went in and started peeling potatoes, that was the end of it. Grandma always moved onto a different subject when she moved to a different location. And I must say, when you move your body, the words get all jumbled. And if you totally leave a room or something, all of the words refuse to come with you. They just stay in that room. Oddly enough, they don't stay for very long. They disperse before you ever get back to them. Lost forever.

Ding-ding. Ding-ding.

Hog came peddling down the street. Didn't even say anything. Didn't even stop. Didn't even look. He just dinged the bell and pointed. That meant I needed to meet him at the Joint. I had convinced him to *ding-ding* when he wanted to talk, and I specified a location, the Joint, as where we would shoot the breeze and talk and what not—like the *ragazzi*. He seemed delighted at the idea when I first suggested it. Unbeknownst to him, doing so was the final measure of my plan to get him away from my house and to cease his hiding in our bushes and what not. When I made it sound cool, you know, like the *ragazzi*, he boisterously accepted.

I looked to Grandma for permission.

She shooed me away. "Just-a be back by-a dinner."

Hog skidded into the alleyway ahead of me. I hammered my breaks and swooped in behind him. If my stomach hadn't already been up in my throat, this meeting would have been uncomfortable. But the thought of what I had done to Hog eclipsed any sign of discomfort and shocked my system with pure, lurid pain. He didn't know that I was the one who had disgraced his whole family.

Hog hopped off of his ride, and I followed him. I adjusted my bike up against one of the fences. When I looked up, he was staring at me, a woeful, saggy-faced stare. We started walking to the Joint in a silent processional wanting usual sputtering of random facts and indecent sightings.

It was really stupid for me not to have thought of Mugga. I mean M, why the hell would I assume Moon? Mugga was around all the time—waiting, watching, looking for Ang, torturing me with his arrogant smile. Of course M was Mugga, of course. But, really Mugga? I mean, he was always "up to no good." But a contract? I honestly never thought he'd be a part of something like that.

I deliberated about whether to apologize. The weight of my guilt was like being yoked to a frost-bitten companion in the wild. Hearing the constant moaning and feeling that constant weight of a half-dead man are enough to put a person over the psychological edge. I just wanted the weight off of me and the voices to fall silent. My needing to apologize really didn't have much to do with Hog, I just needed some relief.

Hog marched up the stairs onto the train platform. He slammed his back up against the siding and stared daggers into the trees. The tranquil sound of rushing water echoed from the banks of the Mahoning.

"I'm sorry," I said.

Hog didn't look at me.

I heard some footsteps shuffle. A man stepped around the corner.

"Ang?" He kind of slumped, like he was ashamed of something. He looked like a little kid that just got caught stealing a pitzell.

Four more guys emerged. Hog sunk back into the crowd.

Moon stepped forward. I'd never stood this close to him, and he seemed much taller than I expected. The thick, rosy ridge of flesh protruded from his neck. Placing his hands on his knees, he lowered his face. His giant nose nearly touched mine. I dared not to move a hair. My eyes stared at his eyes. But I couldn't keep the stare. My eyes rounded, and my focus darted from his right eye to his left eye and then off to the side. The other guys surrounded us. Hog went behind them and stood next to Ang.

"Hog?! Don't you have somethin' to tell Rosie here?" Moon yelled. His hot breath steamed my face.

Hog's rather small, innocent voice trickled from behind the crowd. "Ang was supposed to meet him."

"And?!" yelled another *ragazzi*.

Over Moon's shoulder, Hog gave me a stern glare. His voice deepened. "I'm the one that delivered the letter to your Popi."

Moon cut him off, "You see Rosemary, Hog's been our runner for a while now, and aside from his duties he's been keepin' good tabs on you ever since he seen you slide outta Hyde's with that . . ." His voice took dips and peaks, more disorienting to me than waking from a nightmare. Which, was exactly what I wished would happen. He looked over his shoulder. "Whipped cream, right?" Hog confirmed. Moon continued, "Ya know stealin's a sin Rose," he laughed. His words slowed and voice softened. "We know you picked that letter, picked right outta Ang's pocket. Now we just wanna know one simple thing. How'd the fuzz find out . . . huh?" He grabbed my shirt and flung me up against the Joint wall. "Where'd you take it?"

In that raging motion, a gold chain flung out from beneath his shirt collar. A slender golden crucifix dangled over his sternum. I half expected to see it supported by a safety-pinned chain coming back to haunt me. "Where?" He pressed his fists into my shoulders.

I stole a glance at Angelo's eyes, half afraid of what I'd see in them. Nothing. His glassy dark eyes looked already dead. "Piccolo." The name slipped right out of my mouth.

"The priest?" he asked with a laugh.

Snickers bubbled up around him. Was this who I was now? The betrayer? Nobody was at my side anymore.

"What'd you think he was gonna do? Save us from our sins?!" he hooted.

"Just one," I said. I stared at the chain.

He grew serious. "And tell me this, you know what that stupid little decision led to?"

"I . . . ah, got Mugga locked up." I heard my voice peak like a question.

Moon grabbed my chin and whipped it over to Angelo. "You turned in your own brother's name! Your little act damned him."

I felt the blood drain from my head. I recalled the scribbled message and how Angelo's name was on the letter. With that realization, all of my organs sank down, down, down.

"Never heard of a kid turnin' in her own brother before," Moon said as he sneered over his shoulder. He screamed, "We're the reason you're alive! Hasn't anybody taught you? People 'round here want us dagos dead, all of us. We're just rats to them." His voiced quieted to a whisper. "We're your family, Rosie." He stood back and gestured around him. "Us. You got that?"

I nodded and swallowed hard. "Yes."

"You've got your Daddy's blood. Traitor blood." He grabbed my chin again. "We put him to rest, and if ya don't shape up and stop actin' like a selfish brat I'm not afraid ta drop you in a hole any day . . . Now don't go trustin' anybody else." Moon's hand dropped from my face and he turned around.

I heard a train in the distance as Moon's steps cracked across the platform. Then one of his hands jutted into the air with pointed finger. "As for your penance!" Three ragazzi rushed at me grabbing my hair, my wrist, and the armpit of my shirt, whatever they could get. They dragged me across the platform, and down the stairs.

"No, no-o-o-o-o!" I scratched and kicked and threw myself, but it was no use. They dragged me right through the trees. "No-o-o, I was wrong! Ple-e-e-ase! I won't do it again!" I screamed.

Hog and Angelo tromped through the weeds beside us with not the least bit of compassion in their eyes. You got to excommunicate your soul to do what they were about to do to me. They all brought me right to the edge of the railroad bridge. That's when I saw the evening train barreling down the tracks toward us. The whistle blew bursts of fury, rattling my head, my chest, my left shoulder, my right shoulder.

"Okay," Moon yelled above the raging chugs. "Take her up!"

Ang walked over to me and grabbed the back of my shirt. His grasp caught a lock of my hair yanking my head back. We walked up the steep incline to the tracks and the train came swooping down beside us horn blaring and conductor screaming. The bridge creaked and bounced under our feet as he drug me to the middle.

"Please, Ang, don't," I pleaded.

He threw me onto the ground, taking my wrists in one hand and the front of my shirt collar in the other. His eyes stared into mine—lifeless.

"Please, Ang." The tears streamed down my face.

He moved me closer and closer to train wheels. The wind whipped my hair across my face. Then my stiff body went calm. The thunderous sound of those wheels pumping hammered a soothing cadence. This is it, I thought. This is the end. All of the tension left my shoulders. My arms hung limp, and my eyes eased shut.

Just then, Ang whipped me away from the tracks and stood me up on my feet. My legs crumbled beneath me. Ang reached under my armpits and pulled me back up. Then he pressed my stomach up against the thick steel bridge guard rails. The river flowed beneath us.

Like the voice of a those everyday demons, he whispered in my ear, "Now, jump,"

I didn't move a muscle.

"Jump!"

I climbed under the rail and stood on the edge of the bridge. The worn black toes of my saddle shoes hung over the edge. Moon, Hog and the *ragazzi* watched from the shore. "Come on, Rosie! Show us what your made of!" The muddy water waved with a slow, soft current. And I jumped.

When I got out of the water, Hog was the only one there. Standing on the bank, tottering back and forth in the wind, he studied the river till I made it to my feet. And that's when I got my orders. He told me I'd be a runner for them—no other route but the Line, and somebody would be seein' me.

Wheeling my bike beside me, I limped home. The Italiano Brother's golden age was coming to an end and they saw it coming—resorting to acts of illogical violence and scrapping together what honor they had left. When I swung open our front door, I hopped inside like Angelo used to do. The machete-door slapped shut with a *crack*, but I eased the main door shut. As I slipped off my shoes, I could hear Grandma giggling in the kitchen. Nicky was in there, back from the hospital. He chuckled too, but since his laugh was so much deeper, it got hidden in the walls. My sopping wet, muddy self left a trail down the hallway and I wondered if that guy was still in the basement.

Grandma checked my temperature before I went to bed. I wasn't exactly sure why she did that until I stepped before the grand, bathroom mirror. I thought for sure I was seeing a ghost. My face looked like a kind of a pasty slimy-ball. I looked bad. For me, this confirmed that the nastiness that I felt was not purely due to my having swum with the man-eating catfishes.

Grandma checked my temperature again in the morning and then before heading off to the shoe shop forbade me from leaving the house— precisely articulating, "No leave-a the house," which was necessary. When school was still on and I stayed home sick, I'd never considered that staying home sick subjected me to the house. I'd stay home at Grandma's command, and then after she left I'd leave too, out to the woods. So articulating, "No leave-a the house," was absolutely necessary. But completely useless.

I wandered down the stairs mid-morning to look for some food. The inside of my nose smelled like all kinds of funk. After trying to follow the scent around my room and then around the upstairs, I gave up and started down. Once I turned into the kitchen, I realized that the smell had followed me. I thought that the garbage was going rotten, and then I thought maybe my spinal fluid was leaking into my sinuses. That happened to Char's uncle. I shuddered at the thought, but quickly put it from my mind. I told myself that I was probably getting some whiffs of the insides of my nasal cavities. And I forbade myself to think about the spinal fluid. The basement door creaked when I peeked down the dimly lit stairs. That guy wasn't there anymore.

I turned back to the kitchen. "Rosie." My name sprawled across a note somebody had set on the kitchen counter. It was quite obviously Grandma. One could always tell by her impeccable cursive calligraphy and terrible spelling. I inched closer to read the contents:

Rosie,

Shar cal. Mis you. Sed cal her.

A voice called from the living room. "What are you doin' here?"

Startled, I one-eightied.

"You got the flu, or are you fakin' it again?" The voice was Nicky's. I had thought I was home alone. He was supposed to be at the shoe shop.

I stumbled into the living room, where I found him lounging in Popi's chair fully clad in a stiff, dark-blue onesie. His hands flicked through the newspaper.

"Nicky! What the heck you doin' here? And what in the name of Jimmy Davis are ya wearin'?"

"Work uniform." His steel-toed boots tapped on the floor.

"Work? Since when do ya work? Aren't you supposed to be at the shop?" We never considered our hours at the shop as work. That was just something our family did.

He flicked over another newspaper page before setting it down on the end table.

"Oh man, Grandma and Popi are gonna have a fit if you get kicked out-a school." I nodded my head from side-to-side and clicked with my tongue.

"Can't live off the shoe shop." He leaned over to the coffee table and picked up a glass of milk.

My eyebrows got all knotted together as I tried to work my way through that statement.

"What about when school starts up? Will you quit then?"

He shook his head. "Got kicked out." He pointed to a letter that was laying on the coffee table. "Officially, now."

My jaw hit my chest.

Nicky let out a couple breathy laughs through his nose. "Yep, they really did it this time," he went on.

I snatched the paper from the table and studied it. I was aghast at what I read. "Says you only went to class twenty-three days last year."

Nicky rolled his eyes, while chomping down a five-layer stack of saltine crackers.

"Ha! Unbelievable," I continued. "How'd you miss that many days?"

"Told ya. I've been working at the mill!" he shouted with that you're-a-*gidrul'* tone. "Wouldn't give me afternoon-turn. Said they only need help on daylight. So that's what I been doin'."

My jaw hung open just as limply I as my arms fell at my sides. "Well I guest that's that," I finally responded. "Do Popi and Grandma know you been workin'. . . and you won't go to school anymore?"

He shook his head. "Nah. Just been savin' up a little for us and payin' off the loan that Dad had to take out last year for that turbo repair." We all knew about the turbo incident. It was hard to ignore the engine's ghastly high-pitched scream. He continued, "Suppose they'll find out eventually, right?"

He left the house and I continued my search for food. After knocking back a few meatballs I went back to sleep. They didn't even need sauce to taste good.

Around one, I woke up again. I was awakened by two guys yelling at each other on the street below—something about an unjust game of pinochle. The crack in the ceiling stared down at me. I knew we were losing everything, not just everyone, but everything. And I couldn't do anything about it. Didn't matter whether sin, or blood, or *malocchio*—this was just the way things were, and I couldn't move. I tried to accept that Dad wasn't coming back, Popi wasn't, and neither was Angelo. My eyes traced the eastern seaboard. I figured, maybe if I ignored my fever and aching bones, my sickness would go away.

I lumbered over to my closet and lifted out the box of remnants. The nightstand wobbled when I set it on top of it. I could smell the strong mothball scent as the drawer opened. The smeared photograph lay on the bottom, face down. I flipped it over and dropped onto my bed. Ang's face looked afraid, even powerless. I didn't recognize him, really. To me, he was still that tri-county boxing champion bouncing recklessly around the living room with that mischievous grin spread across his face. Even though his grin sunk and eye's flattened to a muted sterility, when I looked at him I couldn't help but see all that life caged-away inside of him, boxed up by months of misery after misery. I wedged the photograph down into the stack of baseball cards. Then from the drawer, I pulled out the old white envelope and letter and slipped those into the stack of baseball cards, too. *Family is everything* no longer meant what I thought it did when my naive hands pulled it from the crack of the back door. It wasn't speaking of love or honor, but a choice between death or protection. The lid slid perfectly over the sides of the box, leaving not one pocket for air to breathe in and out.

I packed up some of Grandma's gardening supplies, secured the box against my left side and hopped on my bike. The Joint was vacant, no *ragazzi*, no trains, for once I was the king of a place. I took my bike all the way up on the deck and parked it alongside the ticket counter.

When I hopped off the deck, the soft ground squished under my feet, and the vibrant leaves splashed the lingering rain drops on my ankles. I thought that leaving behind the objects of considerable lament ought to provide me some dignity and closure. I finally arrived at the place of the cross—the place where that forsaken crucifix once lain on those damned blue jeans. I suppose that place meant something for me. It was the beginning of everything, my first sin and the opening of my eyes to the dark world around me. There is nothing like the first sighting of your own bad blood, and recognizing the familial inevitability of your own demise.

The ground chilled my knees as I dug a square hole. I made sure it was deep enough that one day grass and flowers and weeds might grow on it. The box clunked as it dropped to the bottom. After the clunk I covered it and proceeded to clean off Grandma's gardening tools in the river. A bird screamed overhead, and I feared for a brief moment that it might shit on me. That happened to Ang once.

The burial felt complete. I felt some kind of rush of significance after the whole shebang, like something was new in my bones, like I could move forward, like I didn't need to be stuck in the past any more.

As I peddled back home, a breeze drifted through my hair and dried my eyes. The gray clouds loomed above with the taunting steel breeze. I figured that I ought to drop off Grandma's trowel at the house before I headed to the shoe shop. I hadn't gone down there in a while, and I was sure that my help was needed, especially since Popi wouldn't be there. Grandma would be all alone, and if I told her I felt better, which I did, she'd likely be alright with me coming out—especially since I chose to come there.

Having dropped off the gardening goods, I cycled down Cascade Street. A smile spread across my face and the shivering bones and blasting fever that haunted me just that morning seemed a distant memory. The day was new.

A curly-haired woman leaned out her window as I rode by. "Rosie!" she yelled, and warmly waved to me. I waved back and continued. A couple of stogie-smoking old fellows nodded to me from the porch where they rocked on their chairs. Despite the steel smoke littering air and pasting gray hues on my faded yellow shirt, the day was fresh. I darted into the alley behind the shoe shop and flung my bike onto the ground, but when I pulled on the back door, it pulled against me, locked. I peered through the window to see if she was in there. The backroom's lights shown dim. I pressed up on the frame, and the window, to my surprise, silently slid open. Nobody was in the backroom and it frail uninsulated wall prevented me from seeing the front room. I was half-way through the window when the front door slammed shut. I froze. Moon's voice thundered, but did not fully obstruct Grandma's slight whimper. Apparently, I had entered undetected.

I lowered myself to the tiled floor which sent a chill through my hands and knees. I crawled to the edge of the doorway and with great apprehension and slowly moved my head around the frame so that my right eye would be the first to poke out—rather than my blind forehead. Moon, Grandma and Angelo stood circling the work bench near the front of the store.

"You-a help us." The voice was hers, her, that once laughing sun that illuminated our house. She slapped a stack of papers onto the bench. "Nicky notta good." She pointed into Ang's face. "You-a one lead our family. You-a one."

If anyone was good, if I could have trusted anyone it would have been Grandma. She tore my heart in two, but somehow it felt lightening. I now could trust no one, but myself. But on the other hand, I felt less alone. All those years I always measured myself up to her. I never knew until that moment that she was a liar, manipulator, traitor and oh so infected like the rest of us. It justified me.

Moon smirked. "Nicky's a coward, just like your Dad was. You know who you owe for your life, and who you outta serve." Moon wrapped his arm around Ang's shoulders. "You-a brother now, and we all got each other."

Ang kept looking down with a stoic gaze. "Why this though? Why do I gotta . . ."

Moon interrupted him, "Angie boy." He seized Ang's shoulders. "You know you gotta get control. You gotta get that money to back you up. You're gonna have some big shoes to fill."

Grandma held Ang's hand. "Popi know-a it coming," she assured him. Then she put a pen in that hand. "We-a need get you in-a place now."

Angelo leaned forward and signed a paper. Grandma immediately collected the documents and stuffed them in a lightly tattered envelope. She handed it to Moon, and Moon handed it to Angelo. They all paused briefly before Ang darted out the front door. Moon nodded to Grandma and she nodded back before he left.

The store was silent. Grandma sat alone poised at the bench. Her dark silhouette cast a murky shadow on the floor. I thought if I could reach far enough, I might be able to touch her head. The shadow jolted, and a crash echoed across the shop. Grandma had spun and hurled a tool at the wall.

At first I thought I might have scared her, but then I realized something else had driven her.

She reached back and picked up a pair of lasting pliers and wailed them toward a picture of Popi and Dad hanging on the opposite wall. It was one that I had taken on Popi's birthday the previous year. She threw a boot and threw a flat and missed three times. And just like that, she dropped her arms to her side, took a deep breath and walked over to the mirror.

I crawled out from the back room so I could see better and stole a glance from around the counter. Standing in front of the mirror, she brushed off her simple plum dress, straightening out the misshapen folds gathered at her waist. Her harsh hands wiped a tear-stuck hair from her stern face. She cleared her throat and began straightening the rows of shoes along the wall. So she hated her life, too? Did she regret who she had become? I don't know, but she seemed to me to be only a mouse—trapped by a heritage of dark choices.

A knock at the door made me jump. Officer Steve Subdolo stood outside and cracked it open. "Everything all right in here?" Subdolo asked. For all his showing up at the right time at the right places, he sure didn't seem to help the cause of justice much. It was obvious that the hot shot Pittsburgh police had sent him up here to check out the situation. Years later I learned they didn't send him to check out Mahoningtown street-dwellers, but the brotherhood's infiltration into the police department itself.

Officer Deleone sauntered passed the window. Just before he moved out of vision, he turned back and gave Grandma an approving nod. She nodded back.

Grandma switched her gaze back to Subdolo. "Oh, come-a in," she answered with a generous flair. "Yes-a, yes everything-a good."

CHAPTER **19**

Subdolo strode through the doorway, awkwardly looking around, and likely searching for something to say.

"How's the business goin'?" is what he came up with.

"Good," Grandma said. She didn't look at him, but continued straightening the shoes.

"Pardon my asking, but how's the family?" he fumbled. "Kids doin' okay after the loss of their dad? And now with Raphael sick, I mean, that's . . . it's just . . . ya know. You have my sympathy."

"We-a just fine," she assured him.

A pause lingered in the air. I tried not to breathe.

Grandma continued, "Rosie and boys, just-a fine. They-a good. They-a good kids. Strong-a kids." She turned and gave a kind smile.

Subdolo returned the gesture. "Good."

I rose from the floor and edged my way to the back window. Silently, I hoisted myself up and began slipping my feet out first.

"Well, just thought I'd stop in. I'll let you get back to your duties." Which was absolutely unnecessary, since hadn't ever stopped her "duties" since he walked in.

"Thank-a you. Have a good-a day," Grandma said.

"You, too."

I plopped my feet on the gravel and slid my back down the wall till I was seated on that rocky ground.

Soon enough, the back door unlatched and squeaked open. Grandma emerged butt first and rotated, garbage bag in hand, toward me.

"Mamma mia! You scare-a me! What you doing back here?" Her eyes looked wild.

I pointed at my bike, which lay slain in the alleyway. Then looked back to Grandma. "Door was locked."

She slapped her hand against my forehead. Her eyebrows lifted "You-a no sick. *Bene. Bene, bene.*" She continued—hoisted the garbage over her shoulder and flung it into the garbage can.

"Need any help in there?" I asked. My voice sounded flat as a pan-a cake-a. Dull. Dissonant. Disingenuous.

"Rosie, what-a wrong?" She dusted off her hands and the clasped them together. "You so serious."

"Nothin'. . . I guess." To tell you the truth, I didn't know what to think. My heart went limp and my mind went blank and it sure as hell was better than feeling the dry-mouth bone-weakening feeling that reality would bring.

"You-a go see Popi. It's-a good." She shooed me over to my bike. "You-a see Popi—room 648."

I swung my leg up over the seat and eased down the pedal. The squeaky door latched behind me. I wondered if Grandma had more meetings planned, and if that was the real reason she shooed me away. How did they expect to do any actual shoe-selling with the doors locking all the time?

A tall pine tree loomed in front of the hospital. Some of its old cones lay scattered on the ground. If I could have found Popi some flowers I would have, but there weren't any decent bushes along the way. After milling around the cones, my eye caught a rather stubby looking one. And for some reason it reminded me of Popi. It kind of looked like him—short, stocky, content. I thought about bringing it to him. But it just looked too much like him. What kind of man would want a picture of himself for a get-well gift? Yea, real cheery. I reached back down and grabbed at a random cone. This ought to do, I told myself. There was nothing special about it. Nothing to remind him of himself. Nothing to make him wish he was the one outside eyeballing all the mysterious cones. That cone was rather normal, that's what made it perfect.

I put it in my leather satchel and headed toward the hospital. I flipped through the spinning door and strolled past the nurses' station. If you look like you know what you're doing, people don't ask questions. Needless to say, I made it by without talking.

Avoiding the opening elevator doors, I proceeded to enter the stairwell. If you asked me, I'd say taking two steps at a time up six flights of stairs is less painful than standing in an elevator full of forlorn and uncomfortable people.

I made it up to Popi's floor. The pine cone laden satchel swung back and forth, still in the rhythm of my stomping up stairs. I reached down to still it, and a tiny spider leapt onto my hand. That couldn't be sanitary, I thought. I flicked him onto the ground and entered the floor of doom.

The sixth floor is the floor that everybody dies on. Nobody formally says that, but you can smell it. You can smell death or near death or fighting death—and smell it thick as steel in the air.

I took my first breath on the floor. The smell saturated my lungs. It was like a sterile cigarette filling my chest and gushing through my veins. But even though it felt nasty, the smell felt comforting—like somebody's name I used to know, but could only recall the surname.

A nurse nodded at me. I continued down the hall. "648," Grandma had said. My shoes clapped on the shiny floors.

"Shoot" I muttered to myself. I had meant to change my shoes before coming. I feared department-store-bought saddle shoes might appear as an affront to Popi's very own nature, nevertheless I closed in on Popi's door. I could hear a familiar voice talking inside.

Angelo. I peeked my head ever so slightly around the door. It was definitely him. He certainly hadn't wasted any time getting here from the store.

Ang sat on a chair pulled up close to Popi's bedside. His thick dark locks were tucked behind his ears and trickled down to the base of his neck. He leaned forward toward a machine and all the wires connected to it. Alarmed by his quick movement, I jumped, but then continued peering around that door frame.

Ang had a stack of papers spread out in front of Popi. He lifted Popi's hand and placed it on a paper. It looked like Popi was having trouble even holding the pen.

"You understand, Popi?" Ang whispered.

A moan came from Popi's lips.

"There you go. This is a wise decision."

Popi's whole body sucked in, and he moaned again.

A rush of chills confused my reasoning. My body trembled as I slid around the door frame into the room. I stole three soft steps forward.

Popi groaned, "He-e-elp."

Ang must have either felt my presence or heard my shoes. He spun around and wide eyes met my gaze. He turned back to the papers and swept them into a folder.

"What are you doin' here?" he barked.

My eyes fixed on the Popi's gray face. "What'd you do to him?"

He glared but didn't yell. "Shut up."

Popi moaned.

"Angelo!" I yelled.

"Shut up," he whispered. Ang sauntered over to me and assured me, "It's gonna be okay, now." His voice sounded soft and delicate, like a mother's to her frightened child.

"What did you do?" I yelled.

He slammed his empty hand around my neck and pressed me into the wall. His fingers dug in. I gasped for breath. Popi's black, fading eyes looked over to us.

Angelo's dark glare surged into my eyes. He whispered, "I did this for you! . . . for all of you." His hand clenched a little tighter. I could feel my face getting hot. "Remember that!"

My head slammed against the wall. I slid across it and plummeted to the floor, propelled by Ang's shove.

Beep, beep, beep, beep. The machine told me what I already knew—that something was wrong. Ang ran to the door, screeched to a halt and then walked, peaceably, out.

Still struggling for breath, I leaned toward the foot of Popi's bed and pulled myself up. The beeping machine flashed a red light and squawked loudly. Three nurses whizzed through the door; others followed them. Their voices all merged into chaos.

"What's going on?"

"Betsy you said"

"Tell Dr. Grazzini!"

"Harry, give me that!"

Hands flew and eyes darted.

"Why is his oxygen low?"

"The machine is off!"

"Who turned it off?"

"Why is his oxygen unplugged?!"

A swarm of wild birds had descended on us.

"Girl . . . girl!" I saw a nurse looking at me.

The room whirled around. Colors and fluorescent lights spun together making a haze of all the details. I could see the nurse move closer to me. I limped toward the door. Every piece of anger. Every memory. Every damned word. Every horrible nightmare wrapped around my lungs. My rib caged cracked at the squeeze. My heart plunged out lava, a fiery biting sting. I lunged toward the door.

"I SAW YOU! I SAW YOU!" My foot tripped on the sea-waved tile floor. My face hit the ground. "I SAW YOU!" And then it was black. My eyelids unlocked and drifted. A face floated above me.

Someone wrapped something around my left arm. I felt a hand on my face, drawing open my eyelids.

"There you go." The nurse turned her head. "She's back."

Someone behind me put a plastic mask over my mouth and nose. I inhaled the best, cleanest, most solid air that I have ever ingested.

Grandma walked in the doorway. Her face looked older—older than I had ever seen it. Her cheeks drooped. The wrinkles on the outside of her curved, making her look tired. The bags above and below her eyes were darkened with a blue-gray hue, and her mouth hung limp, immovable. She wrapped her arms around me and nestled me into herself. Her skin felt cold.

A doctor came in. He told us that Popi was dead. He told us that he would be in touch with Father Piccolo and that we ought to begin our arrangements. He gave his "condolences" and left.

We walked home. The hospital employees offered a ride, but Grandma wanted to walk. So I picked up my bike from under the pine tree.

Gone. Just like that. In the hospital one minute and gone the next. We took a bus across town to city square and the by foot, followed the river to Mahoningtown.

We were silent. My mind just kept counting: one two three four five six . . . one-eighty-two, one-eighty-three . . . three-fifty-seven . . .

I couldn't sleep at that house that night. I just knew I couldn't. I needed to find a place to go.

Once Grandma and I made it to our address, I didn't even go inside. I peddled my way up to Char's. Luckily, she answered my knock. Otherwise I might have just turned back around. When I started off from home, I wasn't headed for Char's, that was an accident—a good one.

I told Char that Popi had died, and I told her how I just didn't want to be alone. She reached out her arms and pulled me into an embrace. Then she pushed me back, keeping one hand on each shoulder.

"I'm so glad you came here. You can stay over anytime. Okay?" She looked deeply into my eyes.

My eyes locked into her gaze. "Thanks."

We moved in the door and kicked our shoes off. The living room reflected a kind of orange glow in the sun-setting light. The TV sat idle in the corner next to her mom's cherry rocker. I never quite got over that chair. I mean, just the regality of the thing startled me to the core. The first time I saw it was the first time I really understood what it meant to worship—and to covet.

"Mom went to visit her sister for the week." Char glanced over her shoulder as she led me from the living room through the dining room. "So Liana and I have to take care of Dad."

Char and I entered the kitchen and found Liana standing over a sputtering pan. Just then, the door off their screened porch slammed shut. Through the lacy curtains I could make out a man, stumbling over the threshold. He fell on the porch bench and began tearing at his shoes.

"Rosie!" Char whisper yelled. She back-tracked and pushed me into the dining room. "Just stay in here. Don't let him see you. He'll go up to bed in a little and it'll be fine."

I dropped onto my hands and knees and crawled under the old Singer sewing machine, which held up her mom's gargantuan and rather dusty Christmas cactus. Under there, I rolled up as tight as I could. Even so, through the machine's majestically intricate iron legs, I could see rather unobstructedly the back of Liana's head.

I heard the back door smash open. Liana jumped. That was a legitimate reaction; I heard plenty of stories, via Char, about her father's drunken wrath. The man wasn't ever really that pleasant to be around, but I guess when he was drunk, it was unambiguously unpleasant. He'd cuss them out and throw stuff, all that. I found it to be a real terrible fate for Char—that sweet creature.

Her dad stomped through the door. The legs of a chair scratched against the floor, and I suppose it was him that clunked down at the table.

"Milk!" he demanded.

Char skirted past Liana. The fridge door sucked open and slammed shut. Milk splashed into a glass. A myriad of sizzles screamed out from the stove, and a big puff of smoke rose above Liana's head. From the sound of things, he guzzled the entire glass in one gulp. Then chair legs squeaked and scratched across the floor. Before Char's Dad even walked over to Liana, a string of obscenities came flying out of his mouth. I mean he was cussing more than a sailor in a storm.

A slight smog had filled the kitchen and began to drift into the dining room. The yelling got thicker, too. The sound of a dish crashing against a wall was juxtaposed with the dissonance of his gravely, stammering voice.

My arms shook as I considered what would happen if he found me hiding, and I squeezed around the back edge of the Singer and propped myself up on an absurdly fat and ragged encyclopedia. For years that encyclopedia had served Char. Seeing that she was so tiny, her Mom forced her to sit on that encyclopedia at family meals. A few years back, Char had stopped sitting on it and started reading it.

I watched as Char's Dad leaned down to Liana's ear and cussed her out, telling her how worthless she was, how she was a nuisance and always got in the way, how she couldn't do anything right. Char stomped up to him from behind. She twisted him around by the arm. Then she jacked him right in the face. I could not believe what I was seeing. The sun paused its trail when the frail, sensitive, hopeful little Char jacked her own father right in the face! That shut him up—that son of a bitch. The remaining sizzles spread out through the silent space.

He walked away. The back door opened and shut, and that was it.

Later on, Char told me he deserved it. She said she had to do what was right. She was kind of afraid about what would happen next, but he was tearing the family apart, and she couldn't just watch anymore.

————————————

That night I dreamed . . .

"Ang?"

His head jerked up. "What?" he snapped.

"Ang you've been so quiet." That's what came out, but it wasn't really what I meant.

I mean his eyes seems a little glazed, like Frankenstein's monster. And his mouth drooped. That's what I meant by "quiet."

He smiled. "I'm okay, Rosie," he assured me. His smile was like a mannequin's smile—dull and lacking the happiness of real-life human muscles around the eyes.

"You used to be happier, is all," I replied.

"Are *you* happy?" he asked.

"I'm alright."

"Then I'm alright."

He finished tightening his laces and walked out to the kitchen. He kissed Grandma on the cheek, said his goodbyes, and chomped down on a good ol' Red Delicious as he stepped out the back door.

CHAPTER **20**

Both Char and I slept late. When we awoke we kind of had a light breakfast-lunch combo made of eggs and grilled cheese with one of those fat, homegrown tomatoes. Around noon I headed out.

I turned onto Elm Street letter in hand, the one Hog had given me at the river, and, saddle shoes tap, tap, tapping the concrete in unison with the creaking gears of my bike, I rolled next to me. In front of the house, I saw Nicky leaning up against his car, cigarette in hand and foot up on the tire like he was posing for something. I tucked the little white envelope into my pocket.

"I'm going over to Tiviano's. Wanna go?" he asked.

I nodded. "Sure." I had no where to be. The Tivianos had converted the bottom floor of their house into a make-shift pizza joint. They lived on the other side of town, but we still liked it. "I'll be right back," I told him.

I traipsed through the door and ran up stairs. The directions I had been given were to put the letter in Popi's nightstand. That, of course, did not make much sense to me, considering the recent event. Perhaps the guy who gave it to me didn't know about Popi yet, though, and I wasn't about to ask him. Never make a man look stupid, or at the least ill-informed. I stomped into Popi's room and yanked the rusty drawer open just a sliver. The envelope glided in settling right next to the shiny barrel of a pistol. I had to use my fists to slug the drawer shut all the way.

Nicky waited against the car, just as I had found him. I hopped in the front seat. As I scooted across, my hand got caught in the torn leather, which reeked with the aroma of freshly skinned and minimally sunburnt animal hide and a gallon of hard liquor.

"What the hell you been doin' in here, Nick?" I demanded.

"Watch your mouth," Nicky replied from the side of his mouth opposite the cigarette. "Damn, Junior. Spilled like a half-bottle of White Satin on the floor, back there."

"Eh."

I didn't require anymore information. I'd seen the White Satin—only stuff Popi would drink besides red wine and the occasional limoncello.

The crisp near-fall air funneled in through cracked windows, which made the air even colder than the actual 61 degrees it supposedly was. My eyeballs started to get real cold, frosted over by that blast of icy wind. And the lids didn't help either. Didn't know who Junior was, and didn't care. If it had to do with liquor, couldn't be anything worth my time. "How's work been going?" I asked.

Nicky shrugged. "Good."

"What do ya do?"

"Build things out of metal . . . been workin' with old Marco Ray."

"Oh, yeah?" Marco was like some old sage of the town—sat in the seventh pew over on the right side.

"Yeah, been real good."

"The bosses like you then?"

He shrugged again. "Yeah, think so. The bosses there can be real asses, ya know. But, working with Marco helps, since he works so fast . . . and keeps his mouth shut."

We drove right along the north hill—in full view of the city in all her glory. A modest strings of clouds drifted across the sky and the mill, too, puffed its own clouds into the air. At the bottom of the hill, two stop-lights changed color simultaneously, allowing the little cars to hum along straight through the city square. Love it when that happens.

We took a few turns through the east-side neighborhood. I didn't recognize any of the houses, since I hardly ever went there. Didn't even know who lived in them. Didn't know if I had seen them around town, or on the street, or at a ball game, not a thing.

At one house a tiny, bug-eyed black boy sat on the front porch railing. His big eyes followed our car from turn to turn. I concluded that he was probably the neighborhood watchman. I know. I used to be own of those kinds. Memorizing license plates, and keeping track of all the buying and selling of goods on the street. Tiny probably ran the show over there. But nobody knew, I was guessing, because nobody paid attention to him, but he probably saved the neighbor's cat from a fatal road-kill situation, and prevented a dozen burglaries just by sitting there staring at people.

Nicky slowed and started to round a corner. I turned around in the seat to see if I could see Tiny. Yep, he still stared. It made me feel watched, but also safe. I knew that kid would have my back if something bad went down on the corner.

Nicky parked along the curb, and we both hopped out. The Tivianos' screen door swung open and clanged shut about fifteen times before we even got to their steps. It was seriously packed out. Three teenage girls sat on the swing, pizzas in hand. Little boys sat out on a couple of stumps in the yard. An old man smoked a cigar in a white rocking chair and just about everyone else and their brother either sat on the railings or wandered about chit-chatting with each other and pulling their jackets in against the breeze.

Nicky opened the front door for me, and we squeezed into the living room. Totally looked like a dance-hall. People were swing-swayin' to the music, singing and talking. It was so crowed that we pretty much were brushing up against somebody all the time—white, black, city-slickers, farm boys, doctors, masons, and even a few Jehovah's witnesses. Nicky sauntered over to the big hole in the wall—literally. Mr. Tiviano had cut this gigantic whole in the wall between the living room and kitchen. I mean it was nice and all. It was kind of like a window right in the middle of a house.

"Yo, Nicky!" a voice called from across the room. "You ever gonna return my ratchet?"

Nicky slowly lifted his eyes to the corner of the room—jutted out his chin. "Yeah, soon as you clean out my car."

I couldn't see around the people to figure out who it was that yelled, but my guess was Junior, given our previous conversation. It wouldn't have mattered if I could see, cause I never seen that kid's face anyway.

Nicky turned back around, "We'll take two slices of Pepperoni . . . Yinz got any drinks back 'ere?"

"We have some Cokes and orange juice," a baby-faced blond boy answered. He was probably about my age. Boys always look and act much younger than girls at that age.

"We'll take two Cokes."

I grabbed Nicky's sleeve, "I'd like an orange juice."

"An orange juice? With your pizza?" He looked at me as if I had asked for a pirogi at a machine shop.

I squinted and gave him a look like he was the idiot. That's how I've learned to respond to these types of ploys. I turned to the blond-boy and cheesed. He handed me the orange juice and that was that.

After paying, Nicky took up our slices and headed for a little two-seater table by the front window, where a couple was just picking up.

I sat down by the thick drapes at the edge of the window. When I knocked my elbow up against them, they released a thick puff of dust, which made me consider what other strange floating particles might be settling on my slice. With my head stooped, I couldn't really see anything down there, but there is always more than what the eye can see.

We chowed for a couple of minutes, and I tried to figure out why Nicky had invited me out—in the past he never willingly took me anywhere. He didn't speak till I had consumed all but the crust.

"How you doin'?" he asked.

"Huh?" I answered.

Nicky stared at his pizza. "Since Dad . . . Popi." He rolled up his slice in the right hand lifting it up to his face. That's the way you're supposed to do it, as eating pizza doubled handed could get you slapped on the back of the head by a close relative.

"I've been okay."

"You've been alone a lot."

"Nah. I go for rides with Charlotte . . . stayed there last ni—."

"And down to the church," Nicky interrupted.

"Yeah. I go down there every now and then. Visiting Father Piccolo."

"What do ya do down there?"

Eyes squinted and quizzical, I rolled up to look at him. "I just go pray. Light a candle. Confess, ya know. Haven't been there in a while though."

He shook his head and rolled his eyes.

"What's your problem?" He was pissing me off.

"Just wondered what you been doin'."

"Ya know, Nick . . ." My pizza flopped down onto the paper plate. "I've been wondering the very same thing . . . What *have* I been doin' exactly?"

"What're you talkin' about?" A bit of pizza slipped from the corner of his mouth. He patted it with a napkin and slid the soiled paper under his plate.

"Yinz need anything?" The little blond kid appeared out of nowhere—as if he just materialized out of the dust particles.

Nicky waved him away. "Nah. Think we're good. Thanks."

There was a long pause. I think Nicky expected me to continue. But I'd learned that it's better to just evade every number of personal questions that you possibly can.

"Rose," a delicate voice whispered. It was Charlotte's, oddly enough. I mean she wasn't there. I just heard her, I guess.

Nicky continued, "What do you mean you don't know what you've been doing?"

"Can't remember."

"You can't remember the question?"

"No, I mean I can't remember. Like remember what I've been doing." Tears welled up in my eyes. I couldn't see my pizza, let alone the dust particles. "I just don't know. I don't do anything. I don't know. I can't remember."

"Whoa, Rose, its okay."

My hands shook. And I couldn't see anything but moving blobs. Nicky wiped his face again and proceeded to stand. He tossed the napkin behind him onto the table. "Let's go," he said, and his eyes gestured towards the door. I suppose he was embarrassed of me. Just me completely going wacko in public was enough to make everyone in the room uncomfortable. I'm not sure how many people were looking at us. Maybe nobody. But I didn't care.

By the time I got to the car, I could see a little more coherently. The world stopped spinning around and stopped looking all two dimensional.

We got in and rolled on down the street. Nicky didn't say anything and neither did I. We sat there looking forward. When we passed the house with the little watchman, I noticed he was gone—no longer at his post. I wondered if something went on. Maybe his dad came home, or worse yet, maybe he didn't. I wondered what his life was like. Maybe he just lived with relatives. Maybe he was an orphan. Or maybe he was a prince—hiding out in Pennsylvania from dreaded wizard, who seeks his death. Who was I to say? But there certainly was something in his buggy eyes that reminded me of myself. Seemed like we knew each other in some strange way. We probably knew each other in another life. I knew about that re-in-carnation. I thought it was like re-incarceration, but it's just in the world instead of prison. Like living again with only a little memory of the past.

"I feel re-in-carnated."

"Reincarnated?" Nicky questioned.

"Yeah. Like I can't remember what happened to me in my former life. Like I think I lived before, but it's more like a dream and I can't really seem to put it together. Just pieces and pictures and nothin' really story-ish. Like a big smash of photo albums without dates or names or anything."

He was silent. He probably didn't know what the hell I was talking about. And to tell you the truth, I hardly knew, myself. I probably shouldn't have been sharing this kind of stuff with him. I knew what they did with people who said crazy things. The same thing they did with Mom. They put them in some Manor somewhere with all the other deformed people, and they shut the doors, and no one talks about them again. And nobody mentions them unless they are trying to insult you. That's how I found all of that out, about Mom. I'm sure Nicky probably knew all this too, but he never told me. Charlotte knew too, because she was there when Mario Siciliano said so. And, I believed him. And I still do. Something in me tells me that it was true. Grandma and Dad just told me Mom died. But no one talks about her life after I was born. They all say "Oh, what a sweet lady. I remember a time before you were born . . ." and so on. Something about me ruined her maybe. Not too sure about that, but I guess I just have to accept it.

"I try not to think about it," said Nicky, jolting me from my thoughts.

"About what?"

"The past."

I paused.

"Sometimes you just can't. You just have to shut it down and get on with it," he stated.

"Get on with what?"

"Surviving."

I could hear the disdain in his voice, treating me like some kind of gidrul' again. I looked out the window and tried to ignore it. The passing trees just winged by, almost to a rhythm. One-two-threefourfive-six seven-eightnine-ten eleven.

We made it home without talking. Now, this was the brother I knew. The brother that I was comfortable with—the silent one.

When we got home, some kind of bustling and shuffling noise emanated from the kitchen. In front of me, Nicky clunked off down the hall toward the noise, steel-toed boots and all. And I followed. We found Ang and Grandma seated at the kitchen table. Stacks of twenties and stray tens lay spread over the table top. Two big army duffle-bags lay open on the floor. Both were about half full with rubber-banded cash.

Nick jumped Ang right then and there. I thought for sure that he would kill Ang this time. I can't trace the words that poured from their boyish lips. Even Grandma threw a fist into the back wall and knocked Nicky's Tuscany painting to the ground. She screamed at me—told me to get up to my room. I stumbled backward and slowly ascended the stairs. A rhythmic thud rumbled in my chest. It wasn't my heart beat, but instead the resonance of Ang's head being thrown into the wall again and again.

I passed my room and drifted into Popi's. The shades were pulled down, allowing only tiny shafts of light through. The nightstand drawer opened with fortuitous ease. I lifted the pistol out—fully loaded—and reached back into the dark drawer for the box of bullets. My fingers had just brushed the edge when I decided that I didn't need more than the six that were already prepared. I left the box and slammed the drawer shut.

CHAPTER **21**

---

*B*ang! Bang-bang!
　　The tree bark peeled back. Those three bullets I shot uncovered its flesh. Even the most knotted trees have got some life. I walked up to it and pulled off some of those bits of bark, but it was clean. No blood stains, as I had suspected. I suppose the rain washes them off trees, unlike its effect on our covered porch, which has clearly sucked in the maroon blotches for good.

Shards poked out around the bullet dents, so I pulled them off, making a fine-tuned display of my work. Something just felt good in me after that. I needed it. It was the first time I'd come down to Covert's field since the incident. Free—I felt as free as the three crows cawing overhead. They spread out and dove down into the field looking for a fresh catch. The field smelled a lot different than that humid mid-summer air that had clouded our vision and frizzed out our hair the last time I was down there. The air was stiff and stale. It stiffened the insides of my nose when I inhaled and was still cool in my mouth when it came back out. Over the bank, the river meandered along, slow, patient, maybe even unaware of all the dying leaves around it.

I couldn't look any longer. The gun dropped from my shaking hands. I turned and started sprinting toward the bridge. Brittle sticks snapped under my pound, pound, pounding feet. I leapt onto the bridge. Those missing slats bore no burden. I didn't care if I fell to my death. Honestly, I think I might have been fine with it.

At the other end of the bridge I took flight, just like those speedy cars hurling out over that steep end-of-bridge slope. I jumped into the weeds.

As I ran, the weeds turned to ferns, that turned to bushes, that turned to trees, that turned to a thick green dream.

I stopped to cross little tributary of the Mahonning. I panted while I scoured the rocky creek for the best route across. That's when the grotto caught my eye. At first it was only a dark mass off to the corner of my vision, but it called my name. Rosie. My own stygian siren. I followed the stream up to a spot where it leveled out a bit and spread wide and shallow. The dark mass now revealed itself to be a stony inlet. I lurked into the dark grotto—over a puddles of stagnant water, broken beer bottles, half-smoked cigarette butts and abandoned candy wrappers—until I beheld a narrow finger of light beaming down deep within the recess. The ceiling fell shorter and shorter with my every intruding step. Eventually I had to crawl, but I made it to that ray.

The beam came shining down through a chimney of sorts. My body compulsively drifted to it with a supernatural magnetism far more compelling than mere curiousity. The vertical shaft tilted at such an angle that crawling was possible, and so I finagled my way up the shaft. The walls closed tighter and tighter to the point that I had to keep my breathing to meager amounts. My feet lifted from the grotto floor as I hastened toward that light. I pushed my shoulders over a ridge that plunged from the wall. It bore into my stomach as I tried to move my hips around it. I pushed and squeezed and sucked in every fiber of my living self, but I couldn't get passed that cool calloused abscess. I stopped—stuck.

After a few moments my moaning ceased, and I just laid my head down on that cold, hard rock. The walls of the shaft were after-rain damp releasing an overwhelmingly fresh mossy scent. I didn't feel helpless, nor afraid, but instead safe, still free, I'd say. A thought crossed my mind: I didn't actually have to go back if I didn't want to. I had the option of never returning to our covered porch, or basement, or kitchen. Never seeing them again. Never having to wade through the thick fear of my own blood. I could forget. And I could be forgotten.

A thin breeze tricked up from the grotto. It freshened the air as it passed around me, reviving the my humidity drenched skin. My lungs expanded and eased back into a relaxing place. The cool wall pressed against my forehead with an alarmingly comforting touch. I stayed there for a while—not thinking, or moving, or fighting just leaning my head against the wall. Then, hot and forcefully, my eyes began to swell with tears. The first tear dripped out, then the second and the third. I remember breaking out into a painful sob. The sounds of my groaning bounced off the walls and filled up by own ears. The tears came so strongly that I couldn't see, and my stomach heaved in and out.

I was safe there, alone and away from the world. I didn't need to be strong. I didn't need to be sober or stoic. Nobody was there to judge my sadness. No one could look down on me, a sad young girl incapable of holding herself together. That was the first time I thought about Dad since he died. What I mean is, it was the first time that I felt for Dad. And, I was so angry that he'd been taken away from us, from me. I pounded the walls and cried. A new wave of sickness came over me. I dropped my arms and leaned my forehead against the wall again. I breathed in and breathed out. "I miss you, Dad."

"God?" I whispered. "Why did you let Popi become so bad? Why did you just let him walk away—into darkness?" I paused. "I miss him, too. I know he did bad things, but I can't believe it all. You know, he was good and loving and he was so funny." A soft laugh breathed out of my mouth. "He was so funny. And the way talked to people, he treated them like, like they were kings and queens. He was so good . . . and so bad, and I just wish you would have done something. He broke my heart. Jesus, he broke my heart."

The stream of tears abated.

A tickle flicked around some hairs on my forearm. Behold, a tiny ant wriggled its way across my mountainous slab of flesh. She descended my forearm's steep incline and with charming finesse stepped back onto the shaft wall. My tired eyes kept glued on that ant, crawling, crawling up, up the shaft. As it neared the top, that inlet of light once again caught my eye. Above, I could see straight out of the chimney right up to the fluffy gray sky.

The clouds lingered up there, unmoving, and then in the middle, a spot began to thin into a translucent veil. With squinted eyes I tried to see what laid beyond, too high for a bird. It grew lighter and lighter every second, until it finally busted down the middle, spinning out into a round window to that vast blue beyond. The spinning clouds formed three concentric circles resembling the lines of an eye. It was as though the sky peered down at me, directly face-to-face.

I gazed into that I eye. The sweet, warm spice of sincerity lay like a mist on my gritty skin. My fears floated on up and out of that chimney. And then came the startling presence. I don't know how else to describe such a movement of the soul except as a flame flickering in a dark room, or trickle of wind rustling a distant curtain. The dark clouds that had swarmed me for months dissipated.

When I gazed into that transcendent eye I knew. I knew that I couldn't let Ang fade away. His shriveling soul haunted me. I finally was able to admit that my brother found his own way into the hands of some beastly spirit. And with the purest of motives ripped an innocent man's life from his body. If I were to withhold my action and bury my memories and ignore that divine turmoil in my stomach I should be just the same as he. What worse blood is there than that of a by-stander watching lifeless eyes fall into the pit.

I imagined Grandma seeing Angelo transformed into a new man. Her eyes would trail to the floor, as she walked to him. He'd wrap his arms around her and forgive her. Sobbing, she'd crumble into his arms. "I'm sorry," she'd stutter, "I'm so sorry."

But, I knew that his transformation would mean travesty for our family. I'd be the token example of betrayal for all the kids of Mahoningtown. But even more worse, it would mean shame. I knew, though, all the weight of it would be thrust on Ang, and he'd consider it the demise of his very own honor. It'd be torn in pieces and bet on by robbers, but there wasn't any other way out—only through that tall chimney into that gazing eye. Everyday that he lived, he kept on getting worse and worse. As I kept on thinking, I wasn't concerned as much about the bad things he was doing, but that warped love he had for us. That propensity to warp love was the bad blood thick in all us Luces, but it got hold of him the worst, split his soul—splintered it apart piece by piece. "Right." Like Char often said. I had to do what was right, and that was all I could do. What is "right" is not always logical, deducible by principles or rules, but it often is a thrust plunging out from a humble soul who sees reality as it truly is.

At the moment, however, I was still stuck, wedged in by that plunging ridge. So, I descended. I couldn't go up to the light. So I eased my way down and plunked onto the grotto floor. When I hit the moss below my feet slid out from under me, and I splashed into the stagnant puddle which released its noxious rank.

I walked back across the bridge, picked up the gun, and headed home.

The box came up rather easily, all things considered. Some passing storms must have settled the soil around it, but virtually no time had passed since

I'd buried it. No weeds or ferns had enough time to take root around it and suck the life out of it like I had once dreamed of.

I walked home and returned the box to its spot at the bottom left corner of my closet. I didn't open it or anything. I just set it in there. Then I went over to my nightstand and slipped the pistol into the drawer. It wasn't like Grandma was going to go searching for it in Popi's stuff. I didn't need to worry.

"Rose!" Ang yelled from downstairs.

I stomped down to him, the vivid thunder of my own steps pounded in my ears.

"Here." He handed me a little white envelope with a red knife-detailed seal. "Take this down by the church. Slide under the halfway-house porch and wait."

I nodded and picked it from his hand. I had to go on as usual until the time was right. I had a strong inclination the time would reveal itself. My bike was stationed next to the garbage can in the alley behind the house. Its rusty chain had infected the area surrounding the gears making it quite a sorry looking creature. I hopped on and peddled out onto Cascade. The seal pressed into my butt-cheek every time I'd push the left pedal.

That's when the thought occurred to me about the first letter. That letter, the one that said "Family is everything," still, I assumed, lay tucked in the stack of baseball cards, right next to the photograph, now at home again in my closet.

An owl sounded a rumbling pipe from a tree in the distance. Yet still that seal in my pocket repetitively accused me of my own treason. It told me over and over again that this was the *malocchio* in me, not a spirit of goodness. But, I remembered the finesse of the ant. There is always a choice.

Looking back, I didn't really know what I was doing then. I mean, everything that surrounded me was too confusing. Everybody was too good and too evil, and I couldn't very well decipher which was which. I felt that the *malocchio* spread its wings over the lot of us dagos, but even in that bitter darkness, I could sense. Angelo was the essence, the human embodiment, of love. He just loved us too much. That's what demented him. He loved us so much that he didn't even recognize he was cursing us, killing us. I had come to the conclusion that perhaps paying the price for his crime might be the best thing for him. In locking him up, perhaps I could free his soul.

I waited under the halfway-house porch. The blond Tiviano kid showed up right when I was about to split. The last thing I wanted was to miss dinner. I handed the letter off to him and got on my own way.

The day after that was Popi's funeral. It was a Sunday afternoon and a small affair. Grandma put a few flowers here and there. Some people brought pairs of shoes that Popi had made. Like forming a kind of garland, they linked them together around the foot of the altar. Men with suits and oiled hair, one being Ang and one being Nicky, carried Popi in and set him with his shoes. Father Piccolo led the ceremony. It was nice. I didn't cry. I didn't even think about crying. I guess once you see so much death you don't think about crying, only screaming, but I was not angry enough yet to let anything out. I was still bewildered by it all.

Though years have passed since, the confusion only dissipated with a languid drip. I never did find out the specifics of what went on between Ang and Grandma. And why Popi had to die. There was only one thing I knew: those papers were critical, by signing them Popi gave documentation that Angelo should receive the inheritance in place of Nicky, the eldest and traditionally supposed to receive Dad's and Popi's as well. The inheritance, in our day, was a kind of symbol. It held the weight of responsibility bearing honor and leadership in our blood family and in the brotherhood, the biz, the mafia. The mafia that dueled with the presiding power and overturned a wicked law system by wicked means. The mafia that tormented any streetwalker who didn't kneel down and kiss their shiny shoes.

A couple of years after I was born when Mom had to be sent to the asylum, Dad left the brotherhood. The thing is, Popi was one of the big time bosses, you see, because when he came over from the "motherland" he needed the brothers. He needed family and, quite frankly, he needed money. The financial demon soon grew into the lord of honor that lorded over us. When Dad was born he was born into it, a first generation brother. When Mom was documented insane and hulled off, something in my Dad changed, something about his eyes saw the world differently and he refused to take care of his contracts and follow his orders. By rule, Popi ought to have killed Dad then and there, but he didn't, for some reason. On the other hand our neighbors and their wives and their kids treated Dad, not poorly, but as though he descended to the grave. To them, Dad was both nobody and traitor. Nicky followed in Dad's steps, not on purpose, I suppose, but due to his natural temperament. Grandma realized Nicky had that rebellious blood—a blood type unsuitable for representing our family. Years later, when people talked more openly of the golden age of the mob and its choking death—of which I was significantly and ignorantly involved with—I learned that Popi owed some kind of life debt to Deleone. Deleone's final grasp at power involved extorting the original families that had wayward sons with help of his first man, Moon, who posed as one of us. He was finally acquitted for extortion of St. Mary's church and attempted homicide, which I am sure was the least of his devilish imagination. Angelo was spotted from the beginning as the one fit to pay for us—prone to naivety and a compulsive payer of debts. They realized Ang was the kind of guy who'd wreck a friend's car, abandon an injured girl in the front seat, and let his brother take the blame.

We rode in darkened cars and blared horns all the way to the cemetery. They put Popi in a hole and covered him up. Dad was beside him, there waiting, I suppose. Maybe it's better that way.

Ladies stood and wept with hunched backs and gloved hands. The men wept too— their bodies like stone, but their faces like those of children. I bet everyone's faces were getting cold.

When people began to leave, Father Piccolo came to me.

"Rose, I, I don't know what to say . . . this is terrible." He rested his hand on my shoulder. "Darkness is a prison. Your Popi and Dad. You can't let your sadness imprison you, your fear, your hatred. You may have it all, but resist. Don't let it have you, all right? The Lord is with us."

The Lord may be with you, I thought, but he sure as hell isn't with the rest of us. His encouragements were just words to me, just pitiful words.

Piccolo gave a concerned look.

"I'll be down to pray tomorrow."

He nodded. "Good."

"I'll need to confess, too, if that's all right."

"I'll be there." He patted me on the shoulder and continued his procession of greeting the people around the grave.

Angelo stepped up to my side and swung his lanky arm around me. A sweet smile spread across his tear-stained face. I put my arm around his waist and gave him a squeeze. Nicky stood ahead of us, across that great six-foot chasm. Hands folded in front of him, he stared at the hole. Nobody talked to him, and he never even nodded to anyone. He just stood there staring. A thin cloud passed over him, making the light shimmer. It moved him from shadow to shadow.

"Ang?" I asked.

"Yeah?" he delicately answered.

"Wanna go look for arrowheads with me?" I tried to sound natural, and I tried to keep my arm soft, carefree.

"Yeah. Let's do that."

"Really?" I looked up to him.

"Of course."

And that was it. He conceded to his fate with ease.

———————

The next morning, I arrived at the church doors before Piccolo had the chance to open them. I waited outside, lying on my back in the cold, dewy flowerbed. The door-latch with its heavy click cued me that he had arrived, but, whether by tired eyes or apprehension, I do not know, I lay there a few more minutes.

Upon my entrance the organ blared out deep, sullen tones combined with dissonant chords. I don't know why the organist thought it necessary to practice at the crack of dawn, but perhaps she just wanted to do her time before anyone else arrived.

Father Piccolo stood at the Mary statue. I walked down the center aisle to my usual spot, but I kept my eye on him. He stood before her with shoulders rounded in humility, yet he leaned forward with a kind of eagerness. I crossed myself and knelt at my pew. The seal of the envelope I had prepared pressed awkwardly into my leg, reminding me of its presence. It's different carrying your own message, rather than speaking the words of another.

The prayers came from my lips with mindless ease and minor contrition. My mind had become fixed rather obsessively on what I was about to do. Worry isn't the word to describe it. It was terror that encased my soul and chilled my lungs and spoke with hasty accusations in my ears. Below the "Family is everything" I had scrawled my own phrase telling Piccolo the place and time. I knew if I could trust anyone, it was Piccolo—a man already wanted dead for the last message I gave him.

I rose from my place and proceeded to the Mary statue. Piccolo did not turn to greet me, but mesmerized by prayer, remained vivaciously poised directly before her. I lit one candle for Dad. I lit one candle for Popi. I lit one candle for Angelo. That wretched, smudged picture glimmered in my mind. I knew that the greatest secret of my soul was stuffed in that envelope, right in front of the letter. Then I puffed out that fiery match.

Eventually, after what felt like three hours, likely forty-five seconds, Piccolo snapped his eyes down to me. "Confession then?" He spoke with an oddly somber tone.

"Yes." I followed him down the long aisle. I initiated our entrance into the screen-less confessional—never had been in that one, and never have since. The wood box smelled like cedar, and seemed to close in around me, but I fought the feeling of claustrophobia. I slapped that envelope right on the wooden slab in front of me and pushed it right over to Piccolo. The dangerously red seal glowed in the warm light.

I jumped out the confessional door and took off running as fast as I could. After taking up my bike, I peddled it so hard the chain fell off right behind the Deleone's Bakery. But before I darted from the confessional, I had said just one word: "Please."

A ngelo didn't back out on me, as if part of him wanted things like the way they used to be. I thought for sure he would recant after that moment of sentimentality had left him. I imagined at least twelve different excuses he might make about why he couldn't go look for arrowheads with me, and I had devised my answers to them. But I guess destiny drags you onward, and all those prayers I'd said for him actually worked.

An invisible weight held down my right shoulder. I dragged it down the stairs, down the narrow path. My limbs shook as I treaded to the front door. Movement through the front window caught my eye.

Angelo sat out on the porch swing, rocking gently and smoking a jack. His arms were extended across the back. The way he sat reminded me of the previous spring when he had won all of those boxing matches. He had gusto, but even more so, regality, like he knew what he was made of. I stole a moment to just look at him through the front window. The haze around the corners cropped him like a photograph. Time moved slower, like a dream— one where you recognize everything and nothing at the same time and your mind just reaches and reaches, trying to find the significance.

Ang's long, wavy, raven-locks perched on his shoulders. He looked out to the road as a car passed. That hair slid over his shoulder so gently. His non-cigarette hand swept the lock back and hooked it around his left ear. The cigarette flicked to the floor, and he just watched it burn out. He bent over it so that the smoke swirled straight at his face. Suddenly, he one-eightied and banged on the window. "What'sa hold up, Rose?"

The knock slapped me out of my dream. "Coming!" I ran back to the kitchen and seized the paper lunch bag which contained my Bologna sandwich.

Ang and I strolled, side-by-side, down Elm Street. The Joint sat idle. No dark-haired young guys lounged around the west-side bench. I couldn't even see the tenant lady through the back window. We hopped up onto the tracks and made our way down the center. It was barely wide enough for us to walk side-by-side, but we did it. We both kept silent. I wondered if he thought about holding me next to the train wheels or throwing me into the river. Only the gravel under our feet knock and clanked and seemingly whispered.

Once we passed the two-mile marker, the clouds began to break. Thin beams of sunlight appearing and disappearing stroked the leaves.

"Been awhile since I been down'ere," Ang said.

"Yeah? Me too. Kinda miss it."

"Yeah. Me too. Kinda eerie down'ere, though."

"Guess so."

A train whistle radiated from behind us. I knew from its sound that it was leaving Mahoningtown and starting its way toward us. My stomach sank. I tried to keep my mind still and silent, incognizant of what I was actually doing. It's probably how Judas felt, when he led those Pharisees and soldiers over to Jesus. I understood him better after that. Judas knew what he was doing, too.

The trees broke into Covert's field. The dewy sheaves waved in the distance, and the enticing smell of night-crawlers perfumed the ground.

"Well," Angelo stated, "here we are. Where'd you wanna start?"

I peered behind him. The train slowly rumbled down the narrow tracks. Its headlight glistened in the sun. "Guess we can start here and make our way down to the river, yeah?" The train's rumbled grew more boisterous.

"Sounds like a plan." His baggy eyes lifted with a smile.

The bright sun blasted him from behind—making my eyes feel the strain and disguising the features of his face. He only seemed a shadow, a form blackened, backlit by the sun.

A sudden loud burst—and Angelo fell to his knees. The sound was clearly a gun shot. Ang cried out, and he rolled onto his side. Someone had shot him in the leg.

"Ah-h-h," he yelled.

I didn't mean for the police to kill him, just take him away, lock him up, be done with it all.

Anger heated my chest. I dropped to my knees and took hold of his shoulders. My throat went dry. Ang's arms shook as he struggled to hold himself up. Blood streamed from his leg and puddled on the ground beneath him.

A figure emerged from the tall grass—pistol in hand. It wasn't Subdolo or Deleone. It was Nicky. And he charged at us. But his face was somber and he flung the tears off of his face as he ran.

Ang looked up. "You, son of bitch!" Using his good leg, he struggled onto his feet.

Nicky's charge slowed.

I screamed.

Nicky went for Ang's legs. Ang just beat him with everything he had left, pulling at his clothes, biting him, wrestling him for his life.

"Stop it, Nick!" I seized a clump of his hair and wrenched it.

Nicky swung around and threw me backward onto the ground. I hit the gravel incline and rolled away from the tracks. The train's invisible wind struck Nicky as the engine passed, allowing Ang to jump on him from behind. I gasped and gasped, but the breath wouldn't come into my lungs, drowning in the feeling that I was about to lose everything.

Nicky elbowed the side of Angelo's head so hard that it knocked him cold. Ang's knees crumpled, but Nick caught him and eased his limp form to the gravel. He placed him down with ease that I couldn't understand—carefully resting his head on the rocks.

I reached forward, crawling my way up the incline to Angelo and Nicky. Nicky had a bandage strapped around Angelo's leg, and was using the tape to secure it. In slow motion, the train chi-chunked past. The engine started to pick up, like the train's internal clock ticked faster.

I'll never forget the way Angelo's eyes stayed open, wide, wide open.

A forest-green duffle bag laid at the edge of the field, where Nicky had run out from. I turned from the boys and heaved myself to the bag. The zipper left a small gap open on the far-side. I reached my hand. Rectangular blocks filled out the bag, making even that thick canvas painful to lean on. I pulled out a block. It was a rubber-banded wad of twenties. When I reached in for another, someone, from behind me, snatched the bag. Duffle in hand, Nicky rushed back up to Ang, who was now waking from his slumber.

Ang cried out in pain and rage.

The train cars flowed past. Nicky picked Ang up, like a baby, cradling him in his arms. Ang's head fell back and wobbled back and forth. Nick carried him up next to the train.

"Nicky! Stop it! Stop!" I screamed.

Both of them were next to the trickling train, Angelo in Nicky's arms, the sunlight beaming down flickering off the pistol. Then Nicky threw Angelo—up, into a boxcar.

An echoing moan pervaded over the sounds of the heavy train. Nicky grabbed the bag and ran along-side the train car. Then he tossed the bag, all of Popi's money, all of Dad's inheritance, all of his honor, his identity, into Ang's train car. A strange provision. He ran for a while, maybe a hundred yards. Just running looking back and forth from the ground over to Ang and back again. Ang's ear rested on the metallic floor but his soft eyes rested on Nicky. The train picked up enough speed that Nicky could no longer keep its pace. He stopped. The train flowed on, down, down, down. Nicky stood there, watching it until it was completely out of sight headed into the West. The churn of the wheels slowly dissipated into the distance, and a light breeze weaved through the grass. Nicky's shadow remained still on the rocky bed. Several birds swept in from the North. They circled above us and swept back into the trees. Silence. Nicky spun around and drifted back to me.

I sat there, unmovable.

"Get up Rose!" He pulled me up by my shoulders. "Come on." He turned to the field and started to it.

I couldn't move. I looked to where the train once trickled.

Nicky turned back to me. He lunged over and grabbed my hand, pulling me into his tracks. We ran through the field. The sheaves sliced against my arms and legs as he quickened our pace. The train whistled in the distance, entering Hillsville.

Nicky dragged me across Covert's bridge and into the forest. The sirens never came. The police cars never darted across the tracks. I collapsed onto the leafy forest floor. Nicky sat beside me for awhile. The train whistled again, on to Youngstown.

"He's gonna be okay, now."

I rolled to look up at Nick, who figited with his lips and stared out at the river. A tear fell from his face dropping onto his pant leg.

"He's gonna be okay," he repeated ,and he kept shaking his head.

Nicky carried me back to the house and laid me in my bed. I woke up—staring at the ceiling, wondering if it was all a dream, wishing it was all a moment of delusion, or some cryptic religious vision.

Piccolo had betrayed me, the directions I left in the note he did not observe. A strange heat welled in my stomach, and its comforting pain inspired me to go, that is, go down to the church. He was supposed to give the tip to the fuzz. Reveal Angelo as a murder and make right the judgement for his sin. I don't know how it happened or what, but after that, I needed to confront Piccolo's hypocrisy. It's like I felt like I should go. I knew it. After throwing my pillows and slamming my hands against the wall and kicking away my box of hand-me-downs, I drew the pistol from the nightstand and strode across the spray of baseball cards that covered my floor. The green super ball rolled to halt by the hinge of the door.

I peddled down Cascade past the shoe shop. It lay silent, trapped behind its now-boarded-up door. A small flock of ravens swooped back and forth above the street. They kept my pace, and I felt as if they were flying with me. Just after that thought, though, they swooped to the left and disappeared behind the houses—houses that in twenty years would no longer exist, houses that became mere, vacant patches of grass.

The sun was setting, eclipsed by the hill in this distance. St. Mary's highest stained glass windows reflected the last rays of a golden sun. I threw my bike behind the bush and ascended the stairs into the foyer.

Holy water.

Upon entering the sanctuary, I noticed Father Piccolo sitting on the front row. I walked down the center aisle. I was so transfixed that I didn't even recognize Char kneeling in the pews off to my left. My eyes stayed screwed on Piccolo, who didn't move. Once I got to the third row, I sensed that he knew it was me.

Piccolo turned his head. "Rosie," he stated in a soft welcoming tone.

The sound of his voice derailed my one-track mind. "Father, I . . ."

"Sh-h." He stood and walked to the Mary statue.

My pattering steps echoed as I joined him.

Piccolo reached into his pocket and pulled out the photograph.

"You didn't give it Subdolo?" I questioned. A bleak haze clouded my vision. "I trusted you. I . . . I, the sirens never came, and I . . ."

"Sh-h."

"Why? You." A bitterness welled in my soul. "How could you?" I yelled. My high pitch piped through the open air. The candle flames bent from the sound. I took hold of his black shirt and wrenched back and forth.

Piccolo took my wrists and slammed them to my stomach, even pushing me backward a little. "Rosie, don't you understand, now?"

I fell on to my knees. Tears streamed from my eyes and sobs echoed. I looked up.

Piccolo took the photograph and rested it above one of the flames. The corner took up the flame. I cried again. When I looked back up, the flame had already erased half of the photo. Angelo, gone. Piccolo dropped the photo onto the cool granite floor, where it finished its burning. His foot smoldered the flame.

I stared, up into his eyes.

He gazed down at me. "You see, his sins are forgiven. You may be at peace."

As the words entered my ears, a blackness filled my vision, and a fiery wave of heat emanated from my core and rushed over my skin. Nicky. Piccolo. They set Ang free, got him out. My body wavered over my knees. I wondered. The tunnel of darkness closed in on my eyes.

When I awoke, Piccolo and Char were kneeling next to me. "What happened? Where am I?" The memories slowly reassembled.

Char's hand patted my shoulder. "You fainted, but you're okay now. You're back." She smiled her knowing smile.

I looked to the ground next to me, and reached to my head.

"Don't worry," Char said. "Father Piccolo caught you just before you hit the ground. Dove right down to you!" She laughed.

Piccolo laughed too and nodded. "Just like in my jersey-wearing, goal-keeping days!"

I pushed myself up into a seated position. I looked into Piccolo's eyes and a familiar face appeared. Jersey-wearing. That day I caught my head in the stair-railing, my imaginings were true. Carmine's son wasn't dead, just like Jimmy Mancini told Popi. Father Piccolo was the hidden son of Carmine. I suddenly realized that was why Piccolo turned in my letter to save Carmine even though the brothers would be after him. He nearly sacrificed himself. Somebody has to pay.

"Charlotte, would you mind walking Rosie home?" he asked.

"Of course I will, Father."

Father Piccolo looked back to me. "Ready to try standing?"

"Yeah."

They helped me to my feet. Char handled my bike as she walked me home.

We didn't talk the whole way. The sky darkened, and the various insects buzzed around the street lights. We strode up Cascade, slapping at our arms every now and again, warding off the mosquitoes swarming in the humid air. The only sounds were bugs zapping themselves into the after-life and our hands slapping ourselves for protection.

We passed the shoe shop's boarded door.

"I can take it from here," I stated.

"You sure?"

"Yeah, I'm all right. You ought-a get back home."

She breathed out a laugh. "Okay, you take a good long rest, Rose." She grabbed my shoulder. "Don't be goin' out and tormenting Hog or something."

We laughed together.

After we turned our separate ways, my saddle shoes tapped on the cement right in time with the squeaking wheel of my bike. Somewhere on that walk, from the shoe shop to our house on Elm, I made some sense of what Piccolo had said to me. He hadn't betrayed me after all. I had thought that paying the price for his crimes was the only option for Angelo. I had figured jailing him would be the only way to gun down his rotting love for us, but punishment wouldn't have made any difference at all. By not turning in the photograph and my note, Piccolo hoped for Angelo. He hoped for mercy. And Nicky had given it to him. Though Nicky should have had all the rage to kill him, instead he set him free. Given Ang a new possibility. That's what freedom is, you see, possibility.

I dropped my bike by the back door. The door was locked, so I dawdled my way to the front. When I turned the corner, I spotted a small light flickering on the porch. It was the distinct orange glow of a cigarette. As I closed in on the stairs, I could see that Nicky was sitting on Dad's chair. The silk swirled up around his head and dissipated into the cool night breeze. He looked over to me and jutted out his chin. I did the same. He looked back to the street, his eyes trailing a passing car.

I walked over to the swing and swayed back and forth. Next to Nicky, Dad's Bible lay open on the stool. The slight breeze lifted one, two, three of its pages, revealing, in its seam, the unsmoked jack—still waiting.

CPSIA information can be obtained
at www.ICGtesting.com
Printed in the USA
FFHW011807091218
49769530-54250FF

9 781532 658600